I0533461

pecan pie for two

A Christmas Romance
Nina Stewart

Published by Legacy Literary House
North Carolina, USA
Cover design by Legacy Literary House
ISBN (paperback): 979-8-218-91529-2
www.authorninastewart.com
Printed in the United States of America
First Edition: December 2025

Table of Contents

Note From Author

Thank you so much for picking Pecan Pie for Two. This story is part of my cozy holiday romance collection that began with Sweet Potato Kisses. Each book follows a different couple and can be read as a standalone, while still sharing the same world, familiar faces, warmth, and seasonal magic. If you've already read Sweet Potato Kisses, you may recognize a few characters along the way. If this is your first book in the collection, welcome. You can absolutely start here.

This is a cozy holiday romance written for readers who love slow-burn moments, soft chemistry, banter, found family, and the beauty of Black love on the page. If you are looking for steamy or spicy scenes, this is not that book.

These stories are novellas, intentionally written to be read in one sitting. They are meant to feel cozy, complete, and satisfying without overstaying their welcome, perfect for a quiet evening, a holiday break, or a quick escape.

Thank you for reading and for spending a little time in this world with me. It truly means more than you know.

With Love,

Nina

Scan to read

Sweet Potato Kisses

CHAPTER ONE

SNOW DRIFTED PAST THE cabin windows in slow, dramatic flakes, which made Wintercrest look like someone shook a snow globe until it begged for mercy.

Rick Franklin stepped inside, shutting the door behind him with a dull thud. Thirty minutes. That was how long he'd been trapped in this Christmas postcard, and he already hated every second. Couples everywhere. Lights everywhere. Mistletoe in places it had no business being. And now the storm had canceled every flight out of town. So much for Tulum.

"Seventy-two hours of this?" Rick muttered, brushing snow off his coat. His carry-on slipped from his shoulder and hit the floor hard enough to rattle the wreath on the door.

He pulled out his phone, the glow lighting the annoyance on his face.

"Uh... Van?" he called toward the kitchen. "Flights just got canceled. Looks like I'm stuck here until Christmas morning."

Sullivan tried not to laugh.

"Guess you're officially part of the festivities."

Rick groaned. "Great. Nothing says holiday spirit like watching couples make out under mistletoe."

Before Sullivan could reply, a voice floated from the couch.

"Oh, don't worry," Asha said, not looking up from her laptop. "I'm sure you'll find something to complain about for the next seventy-two hours."

Rick shot her a look. "And you are?"

"Asha Stewart," she said sweetly.

"Brand strategist. Content producer. Professional vibe checker. Ryan flew me in to film all this holiday magic. I just beat the storm myself."

"Uh-huh," he muttered. "I love that for you." He didn't even try to hide the sarcasm.

Asha didn't miss the sarcasm. Not a drop. She pressed deeper into the sofa, arms and legs crossed; her expression was cool enough to frost the windows.

Ryan drifted past with garland wrapped around both wrists like she was headlining a holiday parade. She beamed. "Oh, this is going to be good."

Of course she was happy. Chaos was her love language.

Fabian, singing "and this Christmas" loud and aggressively off-key, shimmied behind her with a box of ornaments.

Rick, visibly annoyed, rolled his eyes.

"Well, Rick, your room is still warm. Might as well get comfy," Brandy called from the kitchen. She and Sullivan were trying to recreate a holiday drink they saw on social media. The results were questionable.

He still couldn't believe he wouldn't have white-hot sand between his toes tomorrow. He'd been here all week helping Sullivan plan and coordinate this whole Christmas gathering for their friends. The incentive was the trip to Tulum before kicking off Sullivan's twelve-city book tour for A Love Like This. Rick had it all planned: a few days to relax in Tulum, fly back to New York just in time to host his annual New Year's Eve bash, then off to Seattle. But that didn't go as planned.

While finalizing Christmas details, Rick came up with what he thought was the perfect idea: a mini book signing at Wintercrest Books. The town's women's book club loved Sullivan's work, and the club's president owned the cabin they were staying in. Rick negotiated a discounted stay in exchange for the signing. Easy. Van just had to show up.

Rick had zoned out the small woman on the couch until he snapped back to reality at the sound of her laptop snapping shut with the kind of satisfaction reserved for people who are about to cause trouble. Asha Stewart looked up, camera already in hand.

"Try not to trip over your own attitude, Franklin," she said, lifting the lens.

Click.

Rick stared. "It's actually Rick. And how do you know my last name? And... woman, did you just take a picture of me?" His voice carried equal parts, confusion, and pure annoyance.

"No," Asha said, checking her screen. "I took art. And I do my research on everyone."

"Well, I'm not in the mood for a documentary crew."

"Well," she said sweetly, "lucky for you, I'm not a crew. I'm talent."

From the kitchen, Sullivan laughed under his breath.

Asha stood, smoothing her Christmas sweater like she ran the place. Rick watched her the way someone watched fireworks going off indoors. Pretty. Alarming. Better admired from a safe distance.

She lifted her camera again, squinting at the fireplace. The string lights she'd arranged glowed above a mug she'd positioned at the perfect angle.

"Ryan!" she called. "I need a pinecone. Or a sprig. A sprig would be iconic."

Ryan shouted from the tree, "I am busy creating winter wonderland magic. Do I look like a sprig dealer to you?"

"You look like the plug for all things festive," Asha said, adjusting her focus. "Please. I'm trying to create holiday brilliance."

Sullivan walked in wearing a cream sweater, sleeves pushed up, gold chain catching the firelight. He smelled like warm cologne and radiated Christmas boyfriend energy.

"Rick, since you're staying longer," Sullivan said, "why don't you grab what they need? There's a box of seasonal nonsense in the mudroom. Top shelf. Left side. One box labeled 'fall stuff.' Please don't ask."

Asha nodded approvingly. "See? Leadership. Delegation. Specificity."

Rick pressed his lips together, swallowed the response he wanted to give, and headed toward the mudroom.

He made it two steps before Sullivan clapped him on the shoulder.

"Glad you're still here," Sullivan said. "Now you can help make sure the signing runs smooth tomorrow. And Asha is filming the whole thing."

Rick stopped cold.

"She is filming... what now?"

Asha practically glowed. "I pitched Sull a full holiday content strategy. Behind-the-scenes shots. Cozy fan moments. Branded vibes. Aesthetic pie close-ups. Extremely marketable."

Rick looked at Sullivan like betrayal had a government-issued ID.

"Sull? We're calling you Sull now?" he said, laughing in disbelief. "And you let this woman with a camera curate your book signing?"

"I leave for the airport and come back and my job is in jeopardy, huh?" He muttered the entire walk to the mudroom.

When he returned, Sullivan raised both hands. "Whoa, Rick. You know you're my guy. No one is taking your spot."

He motioned to the box Rick carried, leaves, acorns, twine, stray cinnamon sticks. It looked like fall had thrown up inside a cardboard box.

"Asha just had a good idea. A damn great idea that I should be building my platforms. Show the whole Sullivan Harper Experience." He spread his hands like he was unveiling a Broadway marquee.

Rick looked from Asha to Sullivan. Then back to Asha. Her smug smile was practically trademarked. Her short haircut framed her face like Halle Berry in her prime, and her round glasses made her look like a stylish, miniature mad scientist.

Still holding the box of fall decor, Asha's voice cut through the cabin before he could set it down.

"Desiree! Marcus! Stay right there," she said, hopping up like she'd just been plugged into an outlet. "Yes, turn toward the fire. Perfect. Marcus, bring that marshmallow up just a little, cute! Oh my gosh, this is giving wholesome-holiday-rom-com."

Desiree giggled as Marcus fed her a marshmallow on a skewer, the fire flickering behind them like a magazine spread. Asha snapped a dozen pictures, each one hyping the couple more than the last.

Rick watched, unimpressed but painfully aware of how the room shifted around her. She had the whole cabin laughing, posing, rearranging themselves like extras in a Christmas special. She snapped a candid of Ryan and Fabian, then hyped them up like they were supermodels.

"Fabian, tilt your head, yes! Ryan, don't smile so hard, your joy is blinding me." Everyone ate it up.

Rick stood there holding a box full of acorns, cinnamon sticks, and leaf-shaped nonsense, wondering what alternate universe he'd fallen into where he was suddenly surrounded by cheerful adults auditioning to be elves.

Asha turned, camera up, eyes locked on him like he was a piece of set dressing she forgot to adjust.

"Rick! Grab a pinecone from that box," she said. "The little round one. No, not that one, the cute one."

Rick lifted an eyebrow. "Woman, I don't work for you."

"Today you do," Asha said, completely unbothered. "Pinecone, please." Her tone was confident. Charming. Dangerous.

And to Rick's absolute disgust...his body moved before his mouth could argue again. He grabbed the pinecone and handed it over.

Asha took it without missing a beat, adding it to her set-up like she'd just solved world peace. "See? Look at that. Teamwork."

"Don't push it," he muttered, stepping back before she asked him to build an actual Christmas display. He backed up toward the hallway, watching for a second as the group laughed, posed, and joked around her like she was a portable holiday mood board.

Everyone loved her. And Rick hated that he noticed why. She was bossy, yes... but she was also warm, creative, wildly capable, and somehow the glue holding this entire chaotic cabin together.

Rick wanted no part of it.

He turned away, box still in his arms, and headed upstairs.

His room was small, wood-paneled walls, a tiny dresser, and a full-sized bed covered in quilts and matching pillows in colors that screamed handmade in 1994. He dropped the box in the corner, sat on the edge of the bed, and immediately regretted it. It felt like sitting on a padded brick.

He fell back anyway, staring at the ceiling, letting the irritation settle across his chest like a weighted blanket he did not ask for.

Downstairs, Asha's laugh carried through the walls, bright, loud, contagious. Rick scrubbed a hand over his face.

"She really had the nerve to order me around. And worse... I listened." He stared at the ceiling in pure disbelief.

"I should have told her No, do it yourself." He said mocking himself. He heard her laugh again. Loud and happy, like she knew she was getting under his skin.

"Why is this my life," he muttered. He was supposed to be on a plane right now. In first class. Headed to Tulum. Sun. Margaritas. Beautiful women. Instead?

A snowstorm. Mistletoe. Matching couples. And Asha Stewart. She was exactly his type of nightmare, the kind that talked too much, filmed too much, and knew too much. And unfortunately... the kind he wasn't getting away from anytime soon.

CHAPTER TWO

Asha Stewart flipped off her camera lens cap and watched Rick Franklin stomp across the living room like Christmas had filed a restraining order against him.

He moved with purpose, sharp, clipped, irritated. A man who probably color-coded his sock drawer and yelled at slow walkers. The kind who drank his coffee black not because he liked it, but because smiling at a barista would cost emotional energy he refused to spend.

He passed the tree with a glare so potent even the ornaments looked nervous. Asha snorted under her breath.

"Wow. Someone needs a peppermint or therapy."

Ryan looked over from where she was fluffing garland. "Who? Rick?"

Asha didn't answer right away. She was too busy watching him stomp toward the mudroom in those big, clunky boots like a disgruntled reindeer.

"Obviously Rick." She adjusted her camera settings. "He walks around like joy is a tax bracket he refuses to enter."

Ryan tried and failed not to laugh. "Be nice."

"I am nice," Asha said as she snapped another photo, irritation still simmering under her skin. She didn't know why she let this guy get under her nerves. She was the Asha Stewart. Brand strategist. Content producer. People practically begged her to curate their feeds.

But he'd walked in with bad energy and a worse attitude, acting like she personally canceled his flight.

Now he and Sullivan stood in the middle of the living room debating whether she should be curating the book signing.

"Hmpf," she muttered. "Clunky Boots picked the wrong one today." To make her point, she turned her attention to Desiree and Marcus.

"Oh! Ya'll are so cute!" she squealed, loud, dramatic, on purpose.

Rick's eye twitched.

Perfect.

"Rick! Grab a pinecone from that box," she called, letting her voice carry. "The little round one. No not that one. The cute one."

She didn't really need a pinecone. But petty retaliation was still retaliation. She loved watching him squirm. She hated people who hated joy, especially Christmas joy. And coming from the Windy City, she knew cold weather, so Rick's meltdown over being snowed in for a few days was doing too much.

Eventually he stalked upstairs, box in hand.

Asha, finally done taking photos, reached for her camera bag.

"Rick is just... rigid. Uptight. Is he always like that?" she asked.

Ryan tilted her head. "Hmmm. I don't know. I only see him during some of Sullivan's book signings. But you're right, he needs to loosen up."

Fabian nodded as he and Ryan stepped back to admire the fully decorated tree, a sparkly masterpiece with all the bells and whistles of Ryan's "extra fabulous" touch. The two kissed, giggled, and took another photo together. Usually, Asha finds that stuff cute. Right now? She was thinking about him instead.

"Ugh. Just a grinch," she muttered, shoving her camera into her bag. Then under her breath, just loud enough.

"Sullivan's shadow but with less personality."

And of course, that was the exact moment Rick reappeared to grab his carry-on bag from the entryway.

He froze.

So did she.

He stared at her with cold, still precision, like he was filing the moment under Reasons Therapy Should Be Tax Deductible. Slowly, he picked up his bag.

"Noted." Then he turned and walked away.

Asha blinked.

"Oh, that's great," she whispered. "He has stealth mode."

Marcus, sprawled on the carpet with marshmallows, whistled low. "Oh yeah. Y'all definitely don't like each other."

Desiree raised an eyebrow as she stirred her hot chocolate. "Whew, Asha honey, good luck for the next three days. That man looked at you like he just declared war."

Asha scoffed. "Please. I can handle him. He started it."

Marcus laughed. "Well then, he better watch out. You know what they say about girls from Chicago."

Desiree playfully shoved him, and everyone laughed, even Asha. Still... something bothered her. She'd never met a man who didn't like her. Or at least pretend to. She zipped her bag, annoyed all over again, and headed upstairs to grab her charger.

At the top of the stairs, she turned the corner sharply and crashed chest-first into something solid.

Someone solid.

Rick.

She stumbled; he grabbed the doorframe instead of reaching for her.

"Watch where you're going," he said, steadying himself.

She lifted her chin. "Maybe don't stomp around like a linebacker in a holiday cabin."

His jaw flexed. "Maybe don't yell orders at people who don't work for you."

"Oh please, you grabbed the pinecone just fine."

"I did that for the group," he snapped. "Not for you."

Asha smiled sweetly. "Mm-hmm. Sure."

He glared.

She walked past him with exaggerated confidence.

"See ya later, Franklin," she sang.

"It's Rick," he muttered, heading toward his room.

She kept walking, secretly pleased. Yeah. She could handle him. Even if he was already getting under her skin more than she cared to admit. Asha shut her bedroom door and leaned back against it, letting out a long breath she didn't know she'd been holding.

Rick Franklin. Rigid. Rude. Raised-by-schedules Rick Franklin. Why was he the one getting under her skin when she had more important things to worry about? She dropped her camera bag onto the bed, staring at it like it held all her problems. Because honestly? It kind of did.

This Wintercrest trip wasn't a cute holiday getaway for her. It was work. Real work. Paid work. Ryan hired her, flew her out, and trusted her. This meant something special to Asha. Something big. Something she needed to get right.

She was tired of holding her career together with duct tape and prayer. Over 500K followers in social media and she still had to work hard to get PAID clients.

So no, she did not have the emotional capacity for a six-foot-tall, mahogany skinned, clean shaven, man with an attitude and "I hate my life" energy criticizing her job like he knew anything about it.

That's why she pitched Sullivan Harper. This curation would be a big step for her and she wasn't letting "clunky boots" ruin it.

She kicked off her boots, shook her head, and muttered to herself, "I do not have time for some grumpy man with travel FOMO."

But deep down, tucked under the irritation and pettiness...She felt something else. Annoyance, yes. But also, something far more inconvenient. Interest. Curiosity. A tiny spark she refused to name.

She flopped onto the bed and stared at the ceiling. This job had to go well. Her next client depended on it. Her rent depended on it. Her sanity depended on it. And honestly? Her confidence did too.

She'd been coasting on fumes the last few months, patchwork gigs, flaky influencers, brands cutting budgets left and right. She wasn't drowning... but she wasn't exactly floating either. More like awkwardly treading water and pretending it was a vibe.

Wintercrest was supposed to be her turning point. A reset. A chance to prove she still had it. Not... whatever this was. Not getting dragged into verbal combat with a man built like a billboard model and acting like joy was a federal offense.

She rubbed her temples. If she didn't get solid footage for Ryan's campaign...if she didn't show she could handle a high-pressure, unpredictable holiday shoot...

What then?

The fear flickered, quiet but sharp.

Not now, she told herself. This was not the moment to spiral. She'd spiral later, in private, with pajamas and a peppermint mocha.

Right now? She had a job to nail. And a grumpy man downstairs who clearly needed a personality transplant. Rick Franklin? He was just noise. Loud, frustrating, irritating noise.

But even as she closed her eyes, she could hear his voice echoing in her head.

"It's Rick."

She groaned into her pillow. This was going to be a long seventy-two hours.

CHAPTER THREE

Rick lay flat on the stiff unforgiving bed, staring at the ceiling like it owed him money. He'd finally unpacked and changed into something more comfortable, a simple brown quarter zip sweater, jeans, and a brown beanie. Downstairs, laughter thumped through the floorboards. Loud. Chaotic. Happy. A happiness that exhausted him. He checked the weather app for the fifteenth time.

Still snowing.

Still stranded.

Still stuck in a Christmas town against his will.

"Fantastic." He let out a slow breath and rubbed a hand over his face. Tomorrow's book signing? He had planned it. Every spreadsheet, every call, every detail: dates, times, transportation, bookstore negotiations, seating layout. He'd built it from the ground up.

And somehow Asha "The Ghost of Christmas" Stewart had waltzed in with her camera and turned it into her personal TED talk about vibes. He didn't like it. Didn't like how Sullivan immediately agreed with her. Didn't like how the whole group adored her.

Didn't like how her laugh echoed through the cabin like she owned the lease. Really, he didn't like how fast she'd made him feel... replaceable. The truth was, Rick wasn't just Sullivan's assistant. He wanted more.

One of Sullivan's books was being adapted into a screenplay, and Rick wanted a chance to be on the writing team. He'd been with Sullivan for years, grinding, learning, watching, studying the industry from the edges. Screenwriting was his first love, the thing he did late at night when everyone else was asleep.

He didn't care about this specific book signing. He was supposed to be halfway to Tulum right now, but he did care about not looking like he'd been replaced. Especially by someone who curated pinecones and called it strategy.

Rick sat up with a huff. Nope. Not spiraling about her. He pushed off the bed and headed downstairs. The moment his foot hit the last step, the room erupted.

Gabby pointed at him dramatically.

"Well look who survived his seasonal nap!" she said, bounding up to hug him. Her honey locs were wrapped in a high bun, and she was already in a matching pajama set and fuzzy red socks.

"I heard your flight got canceled while Jackson and I were in town," she said, giving him a once-over like she was checking for frostbite.

Rick had met Sullivan's friends a few days ago as they trickled in.

Ryan and Fabian, the luxe power couple.

Desiree and Marcus, loud, energetic, the life of the party.

And Jackson and Gabby, chill, grounded, good vibes all around.

Probably his favorite pair of the bunch.

"Yeah," he said, letting her hug him though pity wasn't exactly his love language.

"Well, we're happy you stayed, my brother," Jackson said, walking over with a glass of bourbon. He clapped Rick on the shoulder and handed it to him.

Rick took a long sip, scanning the room. Everyone looked cozy and festive, laughing like they'd been waiting all year for this moment. And then he saw her. Asha.

Sitting cross-legged on the floor, charades cards fanned out like she was the dealer in a Christmas-themed casino. String lights glowed behind her, giving her this ridiculous halo, like she was the patron saint of People Who Pretend They're Not Annoying. Of course, she knew he was looking. Of course she smirked.

Rick crossed his arms and leaned against the wall, choosing the furthest possible spot from her. Sullivan drifted over.

"Need to talk to you for a sec."

Rick followed him toward the hallway.

"Tomorrow," Rick began immediately, "we're keeping it simple. Book signing, Q&A, done. We don't need all this extra content circus stuff."

Sullivan raised a brow. "Rick..."

"I'm serious. She's turning it into opening night on Broadway."

"She's doing her job," Sullivan said calmly. "And you're doing yours."

Rick shook his head. "This was supposed to be my event. I planned the whole thing."

"Exactly," Sullivan said. "And now she's helping expand it. Relax."

Rick opened his mouth to argue but Asha appeared behind Sullivan like a horror movie jump scare, tripod in hand.

"I can hear you, you know," she said.

Rick stiffened.

She crossed her arms.

"If you've got something to say about my work, Franklin, you can say it to my face instead of whispering in hallways like you're plotting a coup."

Sullivan pressed his lips together, fighting a laugh.

"You can't be intimidated by little ole me?" Asha added, giving him the hardest neck roll known to mankind.

"Okay," Sullivan said, stepping between them like a tired referee. "Final decision. Tomorrow, you two are a team."

Asha blinked. "A team?"

Rick stared at him like he'd lost his mind. "You want me to work with her?"

Sullivan nodded. "Rick runs logistics. Asha runs creative. You communicate. You collaborate. You do not commit murder."

Asha smiled sweetly. "Relax. You'll survive."

"That's not comforting," Rick muttered.

"Get in the holiday spirit," Sullivan sighed. "Now go play charades before Brandy forces karaoke on us."

Asha headed toward the living room.

"Come on, Franklin. Try not to fall apart."

"It's Rick," he muttered.

"Oh, I know," she said, too sweet to trust.

Back in the living room, the group erupted.

Marcus cued up a timer.

Fabian pointed at the two of them.

"Ya'll got the next round!"

Rick reluctantly sat on the arm of the couch. Asha drew a card, stood dramatically, and acted out something that looked like Jazzercise Having a Stroke.

"Elf on the Shelf!" Jackson shouted.

"Correct!" Asha squealed.

She beamed.

Rick rolled his eyes so hard he saw his own childhood flash by. Next, Rick picked a card. He mimed. He gestured. He flailed.

Asha tilted her head.

"Franklin, what in the world are you doing? Are you praise dancing?"

Desiree wheezed.

"Oh my God, he is praise dancing."

Marcus slapped the floor.

"Bro, stop! I can't breathe!"

Rick wanted to walk into the snow barefoot.

The buzzer sounded.

Asha snatched the card out of his hand. "See? This is why you're intimidated by me. You suck at this. Let me see,"

She squinted.

"Free Willy."

The room exploded with laughter.

People chimed in with what they would've done. Rick shook his head and escaped to the kitchen to refill his drink.

Later in the round, they reached for a new card at the same time. Their hands brushed. They froze. Her eyes flicked up, sharp. His chest tightened inconveniently. She pulled back first.

"I thought we were playing charades, not thumb war," she said.

"You touched my hand first. Kinda rough for a woman," Rick shot back, thinking he landed something.

"Kinda soft for a man," she replied, snatching the card.

The group watched them like a tennis match. Brandy leaned toward Sullivan.

"You positive pairing them up was a good idea?"

Sullivan exhaled heavily.

"Absolutely not."

The group finally settled after charades, everyone refilling drinks, grabbing snacks, and arguing (loudly) about who cheated, who lied, and who couldn't act to save their life.

Rick slipped into the kitchen, poured himself another drink, and leaned against the counter, letting the noise roll over him like a wave he wasn't trying to swim in.

Then Jackson's voice boomed from the living room:

"Alright suckas! Who tryna get they heads busted in Spades?!"

A chair scraped. A table cleared. The whole cabin vibrated with sudden purpose. Gabby groaned, covering her face with her hands.

"See. This is why I'm going to bed. I'm not watching my man embarrass y'all tonight."

"Girl, please." Asha popped up like she'd been waiting for this moment her whole life. Her Chicago jumped out instantly. "I'm real decent at spades. You might wanna stay downstairs so you can help him lick his wounds when I'm done."

Jackson nearly flipped the table.

"Oh, hell nah! Let's go then! Pull up a seat!"

Marcus was already sitting, shuffling cards like a Vegas dealer, Desiree leaning over his shoulder giving commentary he didn't ask for.

Asha grinned. "Bet. I need a partner though."

Ryan and Fabian were already halfway out the back door with a blanket and mugs of cocoa.

"Oh, don't look over here, honey," Ryan said, waving dramatically. "We're going to the fire pit to gaze at the snow like normal people."

Asha shoo'd them away, smirking. She didn't look toward Sullivan or Brandy either, they were curled up on the couch in their own rom-com.

Before she could pick someone, a voice answered from behind her: "I got you."

Every head turned.

Rick blinked, wondering who stole his voice box, because he hadn't meant to volunteer. But Spades was his weakness. He could hate Asha all day long, the game was the game.

"You got who?" Asha asked, looking around her like he was talking to an imaginary friend.

Rick stepped forward.

"I got you. We can call a truce for one game. Unless you wanna let your ego cost you a win."

"Ooooooooh!" Marcus hollered, slapping the table.

Desiree cackled. "He talking spicy!"

Asha smirked slowly. "You decent, Franklin?"

Rick frowned. "What does decent mean? In Chicago talk?"

Asha and Desiree burst into laughter that good, familiar, "you had to grow up in the Midwest to get it" laugh.

"It means good," Asha said. "But you are not the best."

Rick gave her a steady look.

"We'll see."

She pulled her chair up to the table, settling in like she was about to coach the Bulls during playoffs.

"So," she said, folding her arms. "Where you from? Just so I know what kind of spades decisions you make."

"Tacoma, Washington."

Asha's eyes went wide.

"Tacoma?! I just knew you were from Philly. Or New York."

"Why?" Rick asked, genuinely curious.

"Because you give grumpy mean New Yorker vibes," she whispered.

He shot her a look.

She winked.

Marcus groaned. "Aye! Less flirting, more dealing!"

"We weren't flirting," Asha and Rick said at the same time.

Everyone at the table:

"Mm-hmm."

Marcus dealt the cards. Jackson clapped his hands.

"Alright! Joker Joker Deuce Deuce. Let's get it!"

Asha slammed her palms on the table.

"THANK YOU. Ain't no other way."

Rick choked on a laugh before he could stop it.

Asha shot him a side-eye.

"See? Washington boy learning something already."

He ignored her, focused on his cards, praying he wasn't about to embarrass himself.

The game exploded immediately.

Marcus slapped his cards down. "Aye let's establish this right now if you renege, you owe three books! Immediately! Don't play with me."

Desiree threw a pretzel at him. "Boy, you can't even count books. The last time we played you was reneging the whole game. And sandbagged us so bad. I'm still mad about it."

Jackson pointed across the table at Asha. "I'm watching you, Chicago. Y'all be sneaky."

Asha gasped. "Don't do my city like that. We don't cheat. We strategize."

"Same thing!" Jackson hollered.

"Difference is I'm good at it," Asha shot back, cutting with a queen like she'd been waiting all day.

Marcus slapped the table. "HEY. HEY. FLAG ON THE PLAY."

"It's Spades, Marcus. There ain't no flag," Desiree reminded him.

"Well, SOMETHIN' illegal happened!" Marcus insisted.

Asha leaned forward, smirking. "Marcus... baby... that's called skill." The table ERUPTED.

Sullivan and Brandy are now gravitating towards the noise. "Don't tell me y'all need a referee?" Sullivan laughed, pulling up a chair to watch.

Brandy right beside him. "I swear y'all just started and already Marcus about to flip the table."

Rick tried not to laugh. Tried and failed.

"Oh, you think that's funny?" she asked.

"I think you're loud," he said.

"And I think you're slow at counting," she shot back, never looking away from her hand.

Jackson smacked his knee. "Oh, don't start that weirdness y'all got going on."

Rick blinked. "We don't have nothing going on. We're supposed to be on the same team."

"Exactly," Asha said sweetly. "Just follow my lead and don't slow me down Franklin."

Marcus suddenly jumped. "RENNEG!"

Asha threw her head back. "Marcus! I haven't even played yet."

"Still feels like you reneged," he grumbled.

Desiree slid his drink away. "No more bourbon for you."

The next few rounds descended into full, unhinged holiday mess: Jackson talking with his whole chest. Desiree threatening to revoke

Marcus's spades privileges. But Asha and Rick? They eventually fell into rhythm. She counted silently. He mirrored her plays without needing explanations.

They talked with their eyes, just enough to coordinate without getting caught. Then the final hand. Asha lifted her last card slowly, theatrically, like a movie villain about monologue.

"Ladies and gentlemen," she announced, "that's book and game baby!!"

She slapped the card down. Marcus's jaw dropped open. Jackson fell back in his chair. Desiree screamed. Brandy yelled from across the room,

"I can't believe y'all let little ole Asha dog y'all like that!"

Asha leaned back, smug. Rick couldn't stop the small smile tugging at his mouth. For one second, they were actually a team. She glanced over at him He noticed her look and her smirk softened into something he wasn't ready to analyze.

Desiree nudged Marcus.

"Dang. They're good together."

Rick pretended he didn't hear it. But he did. It hit somewhere he wasn't ready to name. Asha gathered her cards slowly, fingertips brushing the table as she picked up each card. Instead of her usual cocky smirk or trash-talking victory lap, she simply offered her hand across the space between them.

"Good game," she said, voice softer than he'd ever heard it.

Rick hesitated barely, then took her hand. Warm. Smaller than his. Surprising in a way that tugged at something low in his chest.

"Yeah," he said, the word coming out lower, rougher than he'd intended.

Neither of them pulled away right away. The room around them kept buzzing with Marcus complaining, Desiree laughing, Ryan shouting something from the doorway, but all of it blurred, like they were underwater and the rest of the cabin was a few feet too far away.

Just him. Just her. And that tiny, impossible gravity that pulled them both. They let go at the same time, too fast, like the moment had startled them. But the air between them changed. Brandy leaned toward Sullivan. "You see that?"

Sullivan exhaled. "That little truce might've started something."

Brandy shook her head, grinning. "Sheesh... I hope so."

"Rematch! Y'all cheated!" Marcus yelled from the table.

CHAPTER FOUR

Asha Stewart was up before the sun; because of course she was. When anxiety, ambition, and Chicago grit braided themselves together inside you, sleeping in simply wasn't an option.

The little gym downstairs hummed with an old treadmill, a rack of mismatched dumbbells, and one stubborn resistance band that kept rolling up on her thighs. Snow slammed against the small basement window like it was auditioning for its own disaster movie.

She knocked out squats, lunges, a ten-minute incline walk and a few ab circuits, but every few minutes her mind drifted right back to last night. Right back to him. Rick Franklin. Rigid. Rude. Raised by schedules Rick Franklin.

He irritated her on a spiritual level. The sighs, the muttering, the way he looked at Christmas decorations like they had personally wronged him. Except he had also been a solid spades partner. And that annoyed her even more.

He had read her signals without her saying much. He had trusted her calls, followed her lead, and when she slammed that last winning card on the table; he had looked at her with a spark of something that was not pure hatred.

Respect, maybe.

Or acceptance.

Or just surprise that she knew how to play. She wiped sweat from her forehead and glared at her reflection in the gym mirror.

"Nope," she told herself. "We are not thinking about him."

But she was.

Just a little.

Because underneath the attitude she could see it. The same thing she saw in herself whenever she peeled back the layers. Determination. Hunger. Someone who wanted to be seen. Someone who did not know what to do when someone else tried to step into their lane.

She was not trying to replace him. Assistant life was not in her destiny. She liked being the one with the ideas, not the one tracking flights and suits and media schedules. But she understood wanting your work to matter.

Ryan trusted her. Sullivan trusted her. This Wintercrest trip could be the pivot point her career needed. Online it looked like she was thriving. Five hundred thousand followers. Cute reels. Brand tags. All that.

Reality was quieter.

An apartment in downtown Chicago she loved but barely kept up with. A grandmother helped support back home. A savings account that was not doing what a savings account should do. So yes, this project mattered.

She needed it to go right. She needed the footage to hit. She needed Ryan to be able to say Asha delivered. She finished her workout, showered, moisturized, and got dressed, letting the routine settle her.

Brown puffer vest. Cream ribbed bodysuit that hugged every curve. Camel Uggs. Gold hoops, layered necklaces, a simple bracelet. Short cut styled soft and precise, edges smooth, lashes curled.

When she checked herself in the mirror, she nodded. She looked like a Pinterest board titled 'Winter Cozy Boss Babe.' Cozy, but very much about her business. She grabbed her camera, notebook, and laptop and headed downstairs.

The cabin was quiet. Fireplace low. The smell of coffee drifting from the kitchen. The snow was still coming down so hard it felt personal. She poured a mug of coffee, opened her notes, and reviewed the setup plan for the bookstore. But something nagged her.

She didn't trust that Rick had double-checked everything. Sure, he'd been assisting Sullivan for years...

but he was also packing for Tulum like the book signing was a side quest. If she was putting her name on this?

She needed to see that bookstore herself.

Which meant...

Waking the sleeping dragon.

She sighed, took another sip of coffee, and squared her shoulders.

"Lord, give me strength," she muttered, heading upstairs.

She stopped at his door and knocked twice. The door swung open a moment later. And Asha forgot English completely.

Rick stood there shirtless, toothbrush hanging from the corner of his mouth, damp skin still warm from the shower. A clean low fade replaced the perpetual beanie, making him look...

younger?

softer?

annoyingly attractive?

He wore nothing but black basketball shorts and a glare.

"What?" he mumbled around the toothbrush.

Asha blinked.

Then blinked again.

"Well... good morning, sunshine."

He sighed and didn't bother hiding it.

"Asha."

"Whoa, okay." She held up a hand. "Relax. I come in peace. Ish."

He stepped back just enough to make it clear she wasn't invited in.

She poked her head in anyway.

"I wanted to see the bookstore before the signing," she said. "It opens in a few hours. So, wanna go?"

He walked to the bathroom connected to his room and spit toothpaste into the sink.

"No." he said loud enough for her to hear. He walked back into the room, moving to close the door.

She stuck her Ugg-covered foot between it and the jamb.

"Dang! You wake up an entire ass, I see."

He exhaled through his nose, long and miserable, and opened the door fully. She walked in, arms crossed, taking in the room.

Of course he was organized.

Shoes lined up.

Clothes hung neatly.

A perfectly folded stack of six beanies laid out like they were part of a museum exhibit.

"What a psycho," she muttered under her breath.

"I can hear you," he said.

She didn't stop snooping.

"You don't want to check the bookstore with me because... what? You're scared of bookshelves now?"

He gave her a flat look.

"Asha, I've done a thousand book signings. We don't need to make this extravagant."

"You would have left Sullivan to run it alone," she snapped. "So yes, I need to see it."

He put away his toothbrush, slid on a white T-shirt, and reached for his socks.

"And you pitched this to him," he said. "You didn't think through how you'd get around town?"

"Well, I didn't think I'd need a personal escort," she shot back. "But since you clearly know Wintercrest better than me,"

"Asha." His tone dropped softer. "I'm not trying to fight with you."

That caught her off-guard.

He tied his sneakers.

"Let me get my workout in," he said. "Then I'll go with you. I need to talk to the owner anyway."

She blinked.

"Fine," she said. "But you better not ruin my mood with your grumpy energy."

"Pretty sure that's your specialty," he muttered, brushing past her on his way downstairs.

She ignored the spark in her chest.

Victory.

Annoyance.

Maybe both.

Outside the window, the snowfall intensified. It was thick, heavy, and relentless.

As she watched Rick head toward the gym, she tightened the strap on her camera bag and made her way back to the kitchen. She was determined to make sure everything was perfect with this book signing.

She had just taken a slow sip of coffee while looking over her notes for the hundredth time, when soft footsteps padded in behind her.

Brandy.

"Girl, you up early," Brandy said, yawning and pushing curls back from her face as she reached for the espresso machine.

"Morning," Asha said with a small smile.

Brandy loaded the portafilter like a woman who made espresso the same way she managed emotions: intentionally. "Whew. Last night's spades game took me out. You and Rick? I was scared to blink."

Asha laughed. "He's... so grumpy."

Brandy smirked. "And you enjoy pushing grumpy people off-center."

"I don't even try," Asha insisted. "He just-ugh. He irritates me on a cellular level."

Brandy leaned against the counter as the espresso poured, studying her. "But he also makes you think."

Asha's eyes flicked up, surprised. "What makes you say that?"

"Because your whole face changes when you talk about him."
Brandy fixed her latte with hazelnut syrup and foam. "Plus, I'm a family
therapist. I see this often in couples. Reading people is literally my job."

Asha snorted. "That explains the calm energy."

Brandy laughed softly, took a sip of her latte closing her eyes and
savoring the first sip. She slowly opens them and takes a long look at
Asha.

"Now... what's going on? With you, I mean. This trip matters a lot
to you huh?"

Asha's breath tightened. She glanced at the snow outside, then back
at Brandy.

"My career's just... not what social media makes it look like," Asha
admitted quietly. "Algorithms and budgets changed. I take care of my
grandmother. Medicine and copays are not cheap. I can't afford to miss
on this one."

Brandy's expression softened in that therapist-but-also-your-
homegirl way. "You're allowed to be driven. You're allowed to want
more. Just don't convince yourself you're failing when you're building."

Asha blinked hard. "I-thank you. That... hit."

"That's what I do," Brandy teased, lifting her mug. "Therapy before
breakfast."

They laughed together, and for the first time since arriving, Asha
felt a little lighter.

Then.

Heavy footsteps.

Gym shoes.

The energy shifted.

Rick walked in.

Sweat dampened his face, a towel hung around his neck, and his tee
clung to his chest in a way that felt illegal before 8am.

He paused just long enough to take them both in, Asha at the counter, Brandy sipping her latte before his eyes lingered on Asha's outfit.

Just a flicker.

Just enough.

Brandy grinned into her mug like she'd seen everything.

"Morning, Rick," she said brightly. "Had a good work out I, see?"

"It was aight. Had to cut it short though," he grumbled.

"Be careful out there today," Brandy warned. "Storm looks like it's trying to become a resident."

Rick gave a humorless grunt.

Brandy smirked, backing away. "Okay, you two. Have fun. Don't murder each other. I mean that sincerely."

Asha sucked her teeth. "We'll behave."

Brandy arched a brow. "Will you?"

She left with a knowing smile.

As soon as she disappeared, the room felt smaller.

Rick moved toward the coffee machine, and Asha stepped left just as he stepped left. Then they both stepped right.

Shoulder collision.

A jolt.

Static.

Tension.

He cleared his throat. "You're in my way."

"You're in the kitchen," she shot back.

"That's usually how kitchens work.

"Well excuse you" she muttered.

He poured coffee with the aggression of a man mad at gravity.

Asha pretended not to look, but her eyes slid right to his forearms.

Veiny.

Defined.

Unnecessarily nice.

Focus, girl.

"So," she said lightly, "about the bookstore,"

He exhaled like she'd asked him to lift a car. "I said I'll drive."

"You don't look thrilled."

"I'm not. But I'll go."

She smirked. "Aw. Volunteering? Growth."

He glared.

And outside the frost-laced window, snow fell harder than ever.

"We are gonna have so much fun," she murmured sarcastically.

"Your definition of fun is concerning," he muttered.

She bumped into him on her way past him.

He didn't correct her when she said, "Go make yourself presentable Franklin."

BY THE TIME THEY STEPPED onto the cabin porch, the world looked swallowed by white.

Snow covered everything, the mountains, the trees, the steps, the SUV. Thick flakes whipped sideways, stinging cold air cutting across Asha's face. She tugged her puffer tighter.

"Oh, this is disrespectful."

Rick grunted. "It's snow. That's what it does."

"Oh, wow. Thanks, National Geographic."

Before he could respond, Jackson and Fabian rounded the cabin corner carrying firewood.

"Aye! Where y'all headed?" Jackson called.

"To check the bookstore," Rick muttered.

Asha rolled her eyes. "Because someone didn't reassure me, he had everything under control."

Rick looked offended. "I do have it under control."

"Then why am I here?" she challenged. He opened his mouth. Closed it. The men exchanged looks. Fabian leaned in.

"Be safe! Storm's getting worse."

"And Rick!" Jackson added. "Don't leave her on the side of the road, man! Ryan will never forgive you!"

Rick pinched the bridge of his nose. "Nobody's leaving anybody."

Jackson whispered to Fabian, "Either they're coming back in love or one of them is hitchhiking."

Fabian snorted. "My money's on love."

Asha marched toward the driver's side. "You know what? Fine. I'll go alone."

She took one determined step.

And hit ice.

Hard.

Her foot slipped.

Her hand flailed.

Rick moved faster than he thought.

He caught her by the elbow, then the waist, pulling her upright and into him. They froze. Snow whirled around them. Their breath puffed hot into the cold. His hand stayed on her waist longer than necessary. Asha's voice came out soft.

"I'm fine."

He cleared his throat and stepped back. "See? God don't like ugly."

Her jaw dropped. "Wow. That's bold for someone whose whole personality is ugly."

He smirked. Just barely. "Get in the car."

He started brushing snow off the windshield like it personally insulted him.

She pulled out her phone.

"What are you doing now?" he sighed.

"Content," she said, filming the snowy cabin. "People love storm footage."

"People also love not putting me in videos before 9am."

"You're barely in it!"

"That doesn't help."

They continued circling the SUV, bickering like a couple that refused to admit they were halfway to flirting.

When they finally climbed inside, the warmth blasted through the vents. Rick buckled in.

"Seatbelt."

"Bossy."

"Safe."

"Annoying."

He turned toward her, And smirked. Not a big one. But enough to betray him. Asha swallowed. This was going to be a very long drive.

CHAPTER FIVE

Rick backed the SUV down the driveway, jaw tight, eyes laser-focused on the road. He ignored how she'd tossed her coffee into the cupholder like she owned the car. Ignored how her perfume had warmed the entire cabin with something sweet and soft that didn't match her energy at all.

Nope. Not thinking about that. Asha had exactly three personality settings: talkative, bossy, and even more talkative. This morning, she'd picked all three like it was a breakfast combo. Asha clicked her seatbelt.

"So... do you drive like this normally?"

"Yes."

"In silence?"

"Yes."

"Wow. Okay."

Rick muttered under his breath and flicked on the radio. Old-school R&B drifted through the speakers. Calm, predictable, and non-chaotic. The opposite of her entire personality.

Asha made a face like he'd committed a felony.

"Oh no. No no no. We are not listening to sad breakup music in a blizzard."

"It's not sad breakup music."

"It is literally a man begging someone to come back."

Rick exhaled. "Don't touch my radio."

She touched his radio.

Mariah Carey blasted into the car at full volume, all whistle, tone and glitter.

Rick almost veered off the road. "Turn that off."

"It's CHRISTMAS."

35

"It's NOISE."

She turned it up.

He turned it down.

Her hand smacked his.

His glare could have melted the snow outside.

A radio DJ crackled through the static:

"If you're out in this storm, folks, you're either brave... or foolish. This one's a monster!"

Rick muttered, "Yep. She's a monster."

Asha folded her arms. "Say it louder. Maybe the snow will agree."

"You dragged me into this."

"You AGREED."

He held his response because, annoyingly, she was right.

They rounded a bend, and Wintercrest appeared through the storm. Snow piling high on rooftops, wreaths leaning sideways, lamplight glowing warm through the whiteout.

Even Rick felt something stir in his chest.

Asha noticed immediately.

Of course she did.

"Pretty, right?" she said softly.

He didn't answer.

But yeah. It was pretty.

He hated that too.

WINTERCREST BOOKS

The bookstore looked handcrafted for a Hallmark movie, stone walls, evergreen garland, and a crooked OPEN sign dancing violently in the wind.

Inside, a bell chimed overhead.

Ms. Barbara stood behind the counter, a woman in her sixties with silver curls and a sweater covered in tiny, embroidered books. The exact small-town bookseller archetype.

Rick and Asha were still mid-bicker as they walked in. Ms. Barbara lit up when she saw Rick.

"Well, look at you! Just a sight for my old eyes. How's everything up at that cabin?"

Rick felt embarrassment crawl up his neck. "Good morning, Ms. Barbara. Everything's great. I wanted to talk to you about,"

Her attention slid to Asha.

"Ohh! And this must be your wife!"

Rick choked on air.

Asha cackled.

Ms. Barbara nodded proudly, like the matter was settled.

"You two fussing already, that's marriage energy."

Rick wanted to dissolve into the floor.

Asha stepped forward before he could recover.

"I'm Asha Stewart, Sullivan Harper's brand strategist."

Ms. Barbara's entire face brightened.

"Oh honey, the Lord blessed you with gifts. My book club can't wait to have Mr. Harper here. Come on, let me show you around."

Asha beamed.

Rick let out a short breath and looked away. He followed them through the aisles as Barbara pointed out corners, tables, and display shelves. Asha nodded thoughtfully, fully immersed, she had that focused, creative expression that somehow softened her whole face.

He hated noticing that too. Barbara pointed toward a window nook.

"That right there will be perfect for your camera."

Asha smiled. "Exactly what I was thinking."

Rick muttered, "Of course it is."

She didn't even turn around.

"You got something to share, Franklin?"

"Nope."

He absolutely did.

But not while she was standing there being... her. Barbara's phone rang, and she excused herself. Rick and Asha were suddenly alone between two shelves, the warm scent of her perfume drifting toward him again. Asha crossed her arms.

"So? Do you believe me now? Useful trip?"

Rick's jaw tightened. "Everything was already handled. You just don't trust me to do my job."

"You don't trust anyone who isn't you."

"That's not-"

She stepped closer, eyes sharp. "You think I'm here to ruin your moment."

His stomach pulled tight. Because she wasn't wrong. Before he could answer, Ms. Barbara hurried back, voice shaky.

"Oh Lord... they just declared a state of emergency."

Asha's whole face fell. "What?"

"The snow's too much. Roads are closing. Y'all need to get back up that mountain."

Rick stiffened. "And the signing?"

"We have to cancel. Folks up near Catcher's Pass are already trapped."

Asha's disappointment hit the room like a cold draft. Rick didn't expect the twist it caused in his chest. He touched her elbow gently.

"Asha. Let's go."

She nodded, swallowing hard.

And somehow that hurt him more than it should've.

THE STORM HAD TURNED vicious. The snow whipped and wind rattled the SUV like it wanted inside. Asha finally spoke.

"I can't believe this."

"I told you the storm was bad."

"Oh, thank you for that brand-new piece of information."

"You dragged us into town,"

"You AGREED, Franklin!"

"You don't trust–"

"STOP TALKING WHILE DRIVING IN A BLIZZARD!"

He turned his head for half a second.

The SUV fishtailed.

Skidded.

Spun.

And slammed into a snowbank.

WHUMP.

Silence.

Asha gasped, gripping her seatbelt.

Rick looked over at her quickly, eyes scanning her like he had to count every limb.

"Are you okay?!"

She drew her breath, then snapped, "What did you do?!"

Adrenaline punched through him.

"Oh, it's my fault? Really? You were yelling!"

"You looked away!"

"Because you're distracting!"

"TAKE ACCOUNTABILITY!"

He shoved his door open before he said something he'd regret.

Asha swung her door open, hopping out and slamming it with force. Rick rounded the car, hands shaking.

"Look. Let's try to push it out. Get in, I'll push."

For once, she didn't argue. She climbed into the driver's seat.

"Tell me when to hit the gas."

He pushed.

She tapped the accelerator.

The SUV didn't budge an inch.

Of course.

Rick wiped snow off his face. "I saw a station a mile up."

Asha blinked hard. "A mile? When?!"

"You were too busy talking."

Her jaw dropped.

"Oh. OH. So, you wanna be funny?"

He kept walking, refusing to give her a reaction.

Big mistake.

A snowball exploded against the back of his head. Cold. Sharp. Instant. Rick spun around.

"ARE YOU CRAZY?!"

She hit him again.

He scooped up snow and launched it at her. She shrieked, a bright, wild sound, and he hated how much he didn't hate it. They became twelve-year-olds: She nailed his neck. He got her shoulder. She screamed. He laughed, actually laughed. At last, he held his hands up.

"Okay, STOP. Truce."

She froze, breath fogging in the air.

Rick exhaled.

"Okay. You stay in the car. I'll walk to the station,"

She stared.

"You want me to stay here ALONE? So, I can get kidnapped? Or eaten by a bear?!"

"No one is going to kidnap you."

Her eyes widened.

"WHAT is that supposed to mean?!"

"It means you talk too much and too loud for a kidnapper to survive."

She pointed at him. "You know what? I'm coming."

"Great. Keep up."

"Oh PLEASE. I walk faster than you."

He snorted. "Yeah. Okay."

They trudged forward, snow slicing sideways.

Asha yelled,

"FRANKLIN! WHY ARE YOU WALKING LIKE YOU'RE TRAINING FOR THE OLYMPICS?!"

"KEEP UP!"

"YOU HAVE THE LONGEST LEGS ON EARTH!"

He didn't slow down.

Neither did she.

Side by side.

Bickering.

Freezing.

Irritating each other to survival.

And somehow... for the first time all day...

Rick didn't completely hate it.

CHAPTER SIX

B y the time they reached the gas station, Rick couldn't feel his face. Or his ears. Or his dignity. Snow whipped sideways, slapping them across the parking lot like it held a personal grudge. A flickering sign above the building buzzed in the wind:

WINTERCREST FUEL & DINER

Coffee • Pie • Tow Service (When Dave Feels Like It)

Perfect.

Asha yanked the door open first, stumbling inside with a shiver that rattled her whole body. Rick followed, slamming the door behind them. Heat rushed over his skin so fast his vision momentarily blurred.

A bell chimed. A waitress in a cranberry-colored apron and gray braid looked up from behind the counter.

"Well, hey now," she said with a smile. "You two look like the storm chewed you up and spit you out."

Rick blew into his hands, trying to regain feeling. "We got stuck a mile up. Any chance we can get a tow?"

"Oh honey, Dave's out rescuing half the town right now," she said. "Might be an hour."

Asha groaned. Loudly. "An hour?"

"Take a seat," the waitress said, nodding toward an open booth. "I'll get you warmed up."

To Rick's surprise, the diner wasn't empty. A few locals sat scattered around, farm boots, heavy coats, steaming mugs, the vibe of people who knew storms like old friends.

He slid into the booth. Asha across from him.

The waitress approached with her pad. "What can I get you two?"

They answered in perfect unison.

"Hot cocoa." They froze. Stared.

And then, ridiculous as it was, they laughed.

A full, warm, stupid laugh that loosened something tight in Rick's chest.

Rick pulled out his phone attempting to call Sullivan to let him know the books signing is canceled and they are stuck at the diner.

"Dang still no signal" he said with a huff.

Asha pushed off her puffer coat with a sigh. "I cannot believe I keep getting the short end of the stick."

The waitress returned with two large mugs topped with whipped cream, cinnamon, and sugar.

Rick watched Asha take her first sip, eyes closing, shoulders sinking, a soft satisfied hum leaving her lips.

Something fluttered in his stomach.

He ignored it.

"How so?" he asked, lifting his own mug.

She opened her eyes slowly. "You really wanna know?"

He didn't.

Except he did.

Asha exhaled, staring into her cocoa. "I had a contract fall through with a company I've worked with for years. It was supposed to be iconic. Then an influencer hired me and didn't give me my full payment. I curated her whole event, photos, videos, even a social media posting schedule and they still haven't paid the invoice. She pulls out her phone to show him a few of the pictures and videos. And I need that money for my grandma's medicine. Her premiums are through the roof now. She's getting older and she needs me more now. I'm just..." She shrugged. "Trying to keep up."

Rick blinked.

She continued, sipping her hot cocoa, quieter now. "I'm not some Instagram-perfect businesswoman. I'm hustling like everybody else. But I guess you don't want to hear all that. You... have a perfect life, right? Celebrity assistant? Jet-setting? Glamorous clients? Trips to Tulum" She winked.

Rick let out a humorless laugh.

Perfect.

Right.

"No," he said, surprising even himself. "Not perfect."

Asha looked up.

He took a breath. "I've been doing this assistant thing a long time. Longer than I ever planned. Sullivan is my boy, and I'm loyal, but I expected to be further in my career. That trip to Tulum was going to be my break before another year of hustling. And yeah... I'm good at it. But that comment you made? About me living in Sullivan's shadow?" His voice dropped. "That wasn't wrong."

Her eyebrows lifted in surprise, not mocking, not triumphant.

Soft. Understanding.

"I want more," he admitted. "I want to write. Screenwriting. Shows, films, maybe something that matters. But I'm always having to prove myself. Always coming up short."

Asha's focus softened even more. "Rick... that's not coming up short. That's ambition."

He swallowed.

Hard.

"Sounds like we are more alike than we think." She smirked, taking another sip of her cocoa. He shook his head trying to resist a smile.

"So, tell me why are you a grinch towards Christmas?"

"I'm really not. I love the season. But I didn't want to spend it with Sullivan and his friends. They are cool people but I'd rather spend it with my people. Plus, I always plan a New Years Eve party every year with my friends. Just a way that we bring in the new year and share our New Year's resolutions."

Asha chuckled

"What's so funny?"

"Oh nothing, just thinking about you with friends."

"Ha. Ha. Ha." He said sarcastically.

She smiled a little. Looking out the window and the storm whipping through Wintercrest like it owed it money.

A moment bloomed between them quiet, warm, and fragile. Asha rubbed her hands together, breath puffing.

"Why can't I get warm?"

Rick smirked. "I thought a girl from the Windy City would be used to this."

"Oh please," she said. "Chicago cold is different. This is just disrespectful."

He nodded toward her hands. "Let me see."

"What? Why?"

"Asha. Give me your hands."

She hesitated... then placed her hands across the table. Small. Cold. Trembling just a little. He took them gently between his own bigger, warmer, and stronger. He rubbed them slowly. She inhaled sharply. His thumb brushed the back of her knuckles.

Her shoulders softened. Her pulse fluttered against his palms. Something shifted inside him, and the wall he'd built felt thinner. Her cheeks warmed, eyes flicking up to meet his. He held her gaze. Held her hands. Held a moment he suddenly wasn't ready to let go of. And then the diner door slammed open. A gust of snow. A burst of cold. A loud voice:

"You the two that need a tow?!"

Rick jerked his hands away.

Asha did the same, cheeks blazing.

Dave the tow guy stomped in, chubby, red-cheeked, Carhartt jacket, overalls, and a plaid ear-flap hat.

"We ain't gettin' your car out tonight," he said. "Storm's too thick. But I can drop ya back at your cabin on my plow route. Pull it out in the mornin'."

Rick stood so fast the table shook. "We'll take it. Thank you."

Asha scrambled up beside him, still avoiding his eyes.

Dave waved them toward the door. "Let's go before it gets worse."

Rick grabbed their coats, holding Asha's out for her without thinking.

She blinked at him.

He coughed. "Just put it on."

She did.

Silently.

Softly.

And as they followed Dave back into the swirling storm, Rick couldn't stop the thought: He wasn't cold anymore. Not even a little.

CHAPTER SEVEN

The second Asha stepped inside the cabin, heat rushed over her like a blessing from on high. Her toes felt like tiny soldiers returning from deployment. Cinnamon, brown sugar, and buttery frosting swirled together in the air, warm, sweet, and wildly unfair considering she had just walked through a personal reenactment of The Day After Tomorrow.

Ryan spotted them first.

"There they are!" she gasped, hand over her heart. "The storm refugees!"

Fabian held up a mixing bowl like Simba at Pride Rock.

"We were five minutes from alerting the National Guard!"

Asha snorted. "Relax. We were fine."

Behind her, Rick muttered, "Define fine."

She nudged him lightly with her elbow, pure reflex. He shot her a look, annoyed, sharp, but his eyes softened too fast for him to pretend it didn't happen. She forced her attention elsewhere. Not about to unpack that right now.

Brandy swooped in, warm and bright.

"Oh, my goodness, you two look frozen! Come warm up. We just started decorating cookies."

Asha eased onto an ottoman, dread pooling at the thought of pulling her boots off her numb feet.

"If I take these off, just know there's a fifty-fifty chance my toes don't come back."

"You'll be fine. And perfect timing, we need another team."

Asha blinked. "Team? For what?"

Marcus lifted a spatula like he was about to deliver a sermon.

"Cookie decorating contest: Couples versus Calamity."

Rick groaned. "Please tell me we're not,"

"Oh yes you are," Ryan announced, hands clasped in giddy delight. "You two are Calamity. Since you're not a couple."

"Well dang," Asha complained. "Can we warm up first? We were literally stranded. At a truck stop diner. Walked several miles. In a blizzard. And now you want us to... make cookies?"

Desiree trotted downstairs, lip gloss shimmering.

"Asha is right. Let them warm up. They weren't gonna win this anyway."

"Desiree!" Marcus gasped.

"Just calling it like I see it." She grabbed a drink from the bar.

Ryan softened, touching Asha's knee.

"I'm just happy you're back safe. Take your time, cookies aren't going anywhere."

Rick shrugged off his coat and headed toward the long wooden table overflowing with piping bags, sprinkles, and enough frosting to fund a dental crisis.

Asha watched him go, rolled her eyes, then sighed and pushed herself up.

"Let me guess," she said, trailing behind him. "You can't lose at this either?"

Rick didn't look at her. "I refuse to let Marcus and Desiree win at anything. That's all."

Asha smirked, rolling up the sleeves of her cream bodysuit and removing her burgundy hat.

"Oh, so this is about pride. Got it."

"Ummm, HANDS," Desiree scolded from across the kitchen. "Wash them, please. You two have been in public."

Asha stuck her tongue out behind her back but headed to the sink with Rick.

They returned to the table, freshly washed and slightly thawed.

Rick picked up a blank snowman cookie. "This is why I didn't want to spend Christmas with couples who have nothing to do but bake cookies."

Asha picked up her own. "Isn't this fun, Franklin?" she said before taking a bite out of the cookie's head.

He ignored her. But the corner of his mouth twitched. Just slightly. Enough to make her heart skip. They both reached for the frosting bowl, at the same time, and their fingers brushed.

Asha froze.

Rick did too.

Heat flickered across her chest before she shoved the bowl toward him.

"You can go first," she blurted.

"Thanks," he said quietly, too quietly, his voice warm and rough in a way that made her pulse jump.

Rick piped neat, perfect lines with maddening ease. His snowman looked professionally catered.

Asha squeezed her piping bag... and a blob shot across her cookie like a crime scene splatter.

"...huh."

She stared at it. "He looks like he's seen the gates."

Rick snorted, trying and failing to hold it in.

"You're terrible at this."

"Wow. Encouragement. Revolutionary."

"No really," he said, humor tugging at the edges of his voice. "This is impressively bad."

She shoulder-bumped him, playful, not combative. He didn't move much. Because of course he was made of brick.

But he smiled.

Her stomach flipped. Rude.

"Okay, Mr. I-Secretly-Bake-On-Weekends," she said, grabbing a fresh cookie. "Teach me."

He quirked a brow. "Challenge accepted."

He stepped beside her.

Too close.

Warm-body, soft-breath, he-smells-like-fresh-laundry close.

He guided her hand around the piping bag.

"This is called control. Gently squeeze,"

"Don't mansplain frosting."

"You asked!"

She tried again. It came out... respectable.

She gasped. "Look! He doesn't look traumatized!"

Rick chuckled, low, warm, and it slid straight through her chest.

"See?" he murmured. "You're getting it."

She wasn't sure if he meant the cookie... or this strange thing building between them.

"You missed a spot," he said softly.

She turned to him. He turned to her. Their faces inches apart. Tree lights glowing behind them. Warm room humming with laughter. Everything slowing down. Her breath settled.

And then,

Marcus slapped the table hard enough to rattle the sprinkles.

"TIME! Hands up!"

Asha jumped like she'd been snatched from a dream. Rick blinked, straightening just as quickly. They looked down at their tray. Two cookies. Matching colors. Matching patterns. Perfectly coordinated without trying.

Desiree screamed. "Oh, y'all DONE. Y'all did a joint cookie spread?!"

Ryan pointed dramatically.

"Winners of round one... Rick and Asha!"

The cabin erupted in cheers and teasing. Asha's cheeks flamed, but she couldn't stop smiling. Rick looked just as thrown, and equally unable to stop sneaking glances at her. They'd survived a snowstorm, a tow truck, and a battlefield of sugar. But this?

It felt like warmth she hadn't expected, danger she didn't fully understand, and something good blooming too quickly to ignore.

CHAPTER EIGHT

The cookie contest had ended. Laughter still echoed from the living room. Cinnamon-sugar air drifted through the cabin, soft and warm and a little too cozy for his sanity.

Rick slipped away under the excuse of "checking on something," but the truth was far simpler, he just needed a moment to breathe.

Not the air that waited outside, ready to freeze him solid. What he needed was space. A little distance. A chance to steady himself without Asha standing too close or looking at him like she saw more than he was ready to admit.

Asha.

Loud, brilliant, dramatic, infuriating, and somehow all of that had started feeling less like a headache and more like warmth. He didn't know when that shift happened, but it unnerved him.

Decorating cookies shouldn't have affected him at all. And yet there he'd been, sitting shoulder to shoulder with her, their fingers brushing, both laughing in ways he hadn't in a long time. Real laughter that slipped out before he could guard it.

That was the problem.

He ran a hand over the back of his neck and let out a long breath, leaning against the hallway wall, tucked just out of sight from the cozy light in the kitchen. If he wasn't careful, he was going to start wanting things he had trained himself not to want. Stability. Presence. Someone who noticed when he pulled away. Because Asha, camera-wielding, eye-roll-throwing, tons-of-energy Asha, had this unsettling way of seeing right through him. And the way she looked at him tonight... it scared him more than any storm waiting outside.

He turned the corner into the dining area

And froze.

Asha stood there alone, backlit by the twinkle lights Ryan had strung up earlier. Her camera and tripod were set up on the table, but the tripod leaned awkwardly to one side leg bent like it had given up on life.

She pressed her lips together, frustrated. "Come on. Stand up. You had one job."

Rick hovered in the doorway before stepping in.

"It's broken," he said.

She jumped. "Jesus why do you walk like a stealth operative?"

"I have normal footsteps," he muttered.

"No, you have UPS-package-delivery silence. Anyway yeah, it's broken." She sighed and poked the loose tripod joint. "Ryan wanted more videos of the cabin vibes tonight, but this thing is hanging on with prayers and delusion."

"Let me see."

She blinked at him. "You... fix things?"

"I exist in the physical world, Asha."

She rolled her eyes but handed it over.

Rick knelt beside the table, turning the joint, testing the screws, checking the lock mechanism. Years of being Sullivan's assistant meant fixing everything from wobbly tables at book signings to microphones dying mid-panel. His hands moved without thinking.

Behind him, Asha fidgeted.

"You don't have to do that," she said softly. "I know I get on your nerves."

"You do," he replied.

She scoffed. "Wow. Honesty."

He glanced up at her.

Her gold necklaces hit the light.

Her short curls were soft around her face.

Her eyes, usually sharp with mischief, were... tired. Vulnerable.

It hit him quietly, in a place he didn't know how to shield.

He cleared his throat and focused back on the tripod.

"It's just bent," he muttered. "The screw's stripped."

"So, it's dead?"

"No."

He fitted the legs back into alignment, tightened the hinge, and tested it. The tripod stood straight. Solid.

Asha blinked. "Wait... you fixed it?"

He stood and handed it back to her.

"Yeah."

She held it like he'd just given her a miracle.

"Oh," she whispered. "Um... thank you."

Her tone wasn't sarcastic, or performative, or even dramatic this time. It was honest, simple, real, and it landed deeper than he expected. She looked at him with something warm, something gentle, and he felt his pulse thump harder than he liked.

"It wasn't a big deal," he muttered, suddenly warm in the face.

"To me it is," she said softly, thumb brushing the hinge he repaired. "This job... I really need it to go right."

He swallowed. She wasn't just loud and bossy and chaotic. She was trying. Harder than she let people see. And he'd noticed. Before he could say anything else, voices carried from the living room.

"Rick! Asha!" Marcus yelled. "Come on! Next round is gingerbread house battles!"

Asha groaned and snapped back into her usual sass. "Not them trying to work us like holiday elves."

Rick smirked, just a little. "You ready?"

She lifted the tripod triumphantly. "Oh, I'm beyond ready."

As they walked back toward the group, her arm brushed his. Neither of them pulled away.

CHAPTER NINE

The cabin was full of warm noise again, laughter, frosting wars, the metallic clink of gingerbread decorations scattering across the table but Asha slipped away for a moment to rinse icing off her fingers. She thought about going upstairs and changing into something more comfortable but that's when she heard it.

Low voices.

Muted tension.

Coming from the hallway near the back porch. She almost ignored it. She was tired, sugared-out, and extremely close to a cookie-induced coma, but one of those voices belonged to Rick. Which meant she definitely wasn't ignoring it.

She moved quietly, not stealthy like him (nobody walked that silently on purpose), but lightly enough to catch the tail end of Sullivan's sentence.

"-it's just not the right time, Rick. You're stretched thin. Maybe after the tour."

Asha paused behind the corner.

Rick stood with his arms crossed, exhaustion radiating off him even though he was trying to look composed. Snowflakes clung to his beanie from the quick run he and Marcus had just made to the woodshed. His jaw was clenched, his eyes tight.

"This is the third time you've said that," Rick said, voice low. Not angry. Just... worn. "You keep telling me later. I've been doing this assistant thing for years, Sull. I know your schedule, your voice, your cues, your audience-hell, I know your coffee order better than you do."

Sullivan scrubbed a hand over the back of his neck. "I'm not saying you aren't capable."

"Then what are you saying?" Rick muttered. "Because it feels like you don't trust me to do more. If this screenplay is getting written, if someone's adapting your book... I want a shot. A real one. Not a 'maybe next time.'"

Asha's breath snagged.

Rick wasn't just grumpy.

He was burning out.

Working too hard.

Trying too much.

Trying alone.

Sullivan sighed. "Rick... you just need rest, man. You haven't stopped in months. You planned the entire Wintercrest event, you handled every bookstore negotiation, you tracked every travel detail. You're,"

"Doing my job," Rick said sharply. Then softer: "And I'm good at it. But I'm capable of more."

That last sentence cracked something inside Asha, because she'd said a version of it herself, alone in her apartment, more times than she could count.

She stepped forward before she could talk herself out of it.

"Sullivan?" she said gently.

Both men turned. Rick's face changed instantly, guarded, prickly, defensive.

"Not now, Asha," he muttered.

She ignored him.

"Sullivan," she said again, "he's not wrong."

Sullivan blinked in surprise. "You heard all that?"

"Only the part where you're pretending, he isn't one of the hardest-working people on earth." She softened her voice. "He showed up today when it counted. He drove in the snow. He helped troubleshoot everything. He fixed my tripod without me asking, and honestly, I've never seen someone so committed to making sure things don't fall apart."

Rick's eyes widened just slightly, like he wasn't sure how to absorb someone taking his side.

She continued:

"He's not a machine. He deserves rest. But he also deserves a real chance to grow."

She looked at Rick now. "You should want that for yourself. And you're allowed to say it out loud."

Sullivan exhaled, shoulders dropping.

"Asha..." he said, half-impressed. "You're right. I wasn't trying to dismiss him. I just" He turned back to Rick. "I worry about you burning out."

Rick swallowed. Hard.

Asha knew that swallow.

It was the one people used when they were forcing down years of holding-it-together.

"I get it," Rick said quietly. "But I'm still asking for a shot."

Sullivan nodded. A real one this time. "Okay. We'll talk after the holidays. Seriously talk."

Rick looked stunned. Not happy. Not relieved. Just... stunned.

Asha stepped back, unsure what to do with the tightness in her own chest.

He walked off toward the kitchen.

Rick stood there a beat longer.

Asha started to turn away to give him privacy when his voice stopped her.

"...Why'd you do that?" he asked quietly.

She glanced over her shoulder. "Do what?"

"Defend me."

She shrugged, softening. "Because you deserved it."

Rick met her eyes and didn't look away.

Warmth spread through her so quickly it startled her. She felt exposed for a moment. Open in a way she didn't usually allow herself to be. A feeling that came from standing just a little too close to a bonfire; dangerous, comforting, and impossible to step away from.

Rick nodded once, slow, and sincere.

"Thank you," he said.

Asha started toward the dining room, clearly trying to melt back into the holiday mayhem. But halfway there, she hesitated. She turned, slow, unsure, her eyes meeting his like she wasn't quite ready to walk away.

No walls, no sarcasm. Just the quiet stillness of someone who isn't used to being defended and didn't know what to do with the feeling. She pressed her lips together and shook her head once, more to herself than him, before turning away. The glow of the fireplace and the hum of the group pulled her back into the noise and comfort.

Rick didn't say anything.

He didn't have to.

That tiny shift in his expression, a softness she'd never seen from him, was enough to make her heart dip recklessly.

CHAPTER TEN

The storm outside didn't show any signs of stopping, thick waves of snow dancing across the windows like someone shook a snow globe too hard. Wintercrest was locked down for the night. Inside, though, the warmth was loud.

Marcus and Jackson were waging war in the living room, Uno cards slapping the table like percussion. Desiree narrated the match from the couch with the confidence of a sports commentator who'd seen too much.

Near the fireplace, Sullivan, Brandy, and Gabby sat close together, speaking in the soft, intimate tones of people who'd lived real life and carried stories worth telling. The fire reflected warmly across their faces, making the whole scene feel like a commercial for "togetherness" he'd accidentally wandered into.

Fabian and Ryan were turning the staircase landing into yet another faux snow photoshoot. They posed, giggled, tossed handfuls of faux flakes, and insisted they needed "one more" shot every five seconds.

It was busy. Soft, lived-in chaos. Rick stood near the back of the room, arms crossed, letting all of it unfold without him. He was used to being in the background, handling things, watching everything, staying out of the spotlight.

But tonight, he wasn't watching the group first. He kept finding his eyes drifting toward her.

Asha.

She moved easily through the room, camera in her hands, capturing the small candid moments. She crouched to record Jackson accusing Marcus of cheating. She panned across the fireplace where Brandy laughed at something Sullivan whispered. She caught Ryan and Fabian mid-spin, their faux snow falling around them like confetti.

Every time someone smiled into the lens, she smiled back. Every time she laughed, something inside him warmed in a way he couldn't quite shake off. She didn't see him watching her. She never looked his way first. And maybe that was why he kept looking.

Asha drifted closer to the windows, the firelight softening the edges of her face. When she lifted her camera to film the snowfall outside, her breath fogged the glass. For a moment, she was perfectly still, captivated by the storm like it wasn't trapping them but protecting something fragile inside the cabin.

He didn't move toward her on purpose. But somehow, his steps carried him in her direction. When she sensed him near, she lowered the camera slightly. Not all the way, just enough to acknowledge him without breaking the moment.

"You okay?" she asked quietly, glancing at him from the corner of her eye.

He nodded. "Yeah."

It should have ended there. A normal answer. Nothing more. But she kept looking at him, and suddenly he felt seen in a way that made his chest tighten.

"You sure?" she murmured, softer this time. "Because earlier... that was a lot."

Rick swallowed. He didn't talk about what happened in the hallway. He didn't talk about wanting more. He didn't talk about anything personal, with anybody.

But Asha's voice had a way of pressing gently on locked doors he thought he'd sealed years ago.

"I'm fine," he said, but the words came out low and real, stripped of the edge he normally used with her.

She nodded, accepting it without pushing.

Her eyes lingered a beat longer, warm and searching, and for one terrifying second, he wondered if she could see all the way into him-into the long hours, the frustration, the dreams he kept tucked away because they didn't fit neatly into someone else's schedule.

He looked away first.

Asha lifted her camera again, filming the fireplace now, capturing Brandy wiping her eyes after something Sullivan said. It was tender, quiet, and probably something Asha would edit into a highlight reel later.

Rick wasn't a sentimental person, but he couldn't deny it, she saw people. Really saw them. And now she'd seen him. He cleared his throat and stepped back, putting a few feet between them before he forgot how to breathe properly. "You, uh... you're good at that."

She paused, lowering her camera again. "At what?"

"Finding the moments." His voice felt strangely unsteady. "The ones people don't notice unless someone shows them."

Her expression softened, surprised. "Thank you, Rick."

Hearing his name in her voice almost undid him.

Ryan shouted from across the room, "ASHAAA! Come get this! Fabian's about to fall off the stairs!"

Fabian yelled, "I'M FINE...wait, nope. RYAN, HELP!"

Asha laughed, the sound bright and warm, and hurried off to film the madness.

Rick watched her go, feeling something in his chest tilt slowly, quietly, and decisively. He didn't want this feeling. He didn't trust it. But he also couldn't ignore the way the room felt different when she was in it... and especially when she looked back at him like she had any right to see straight through him.

He turned back toward the window, hoping the cold outside might cool whatever was heating up under his skin. But even with the storm raging just inches away, Asha's warmth lingered. And he finally admitted it, just to himself, in the quiet where no one else could hear: He wasn't nearly as snow proof as he thought.

CHAPTER ELEVEN

Christmas Eve mornings always carried a strange softness. Even in a crowded cabin, with a storm piling fresh snow against the windows and nine adults under one roof, there was something peaceful about waking up before the noise began.

Rick had hoped to wake up in Tulum today. Warm sun. Salt air. Sand hot enough to sting the bottoms of his feet. Instead, the cabin smelled like nutmeg, brown sugar, and a quiet sense of home. He wasn't sure which part annoyed him more.

Music drifted softly from the living room, some old, soulful Christmas playlist that made the whole house feel slower, gentler. Snow fell steadily outside. The kind that made Wintercrest feel like its own world.

And for the first time since the blizzard started, Rick didn't mind it.

He sat at the kitchen counter with a bowl of pecans, cracking the shells with mechanical precision. It was a job he'd volunteered for, partly because Brandy asked, partly because the smell of pecan pie always reminded him of the trips, he took to visit distant relatives in Georgia when he was little. Back when the world was messy but simple. Back when relationships didn't feel like traps and future plans weren't something he had to wrestle with.

Brandy stood at the island wearing a flour-dusted apron and a scarf wrapped over her curls, stirring the pie filling in a large bowl. She glanced at him without lifting her head.

"You know," she said, "you're cracking those like they committed a crime."

Rick shrugged. "They might have."

"Mmhmm." The way she hummed made it sound like she already knew everything he was refusing to say.

He passed her the cinnamon without her asking. Years of assisting Sullivan had trained him to move before anyone voiced a need. Help first. Think later.

Brandy noticed immediately.

"See? You do that with everybody."

"Do what?"

"Take care of people like it's your job." She stirred the mixture, tasted it, then added a touch more brown sugar. "And then pretend you don't need anything in return."

Rick looked down at the half-cracked pecans. "I'm fine."

Brandy met his gaze with the look trained professionals reserved for clients who believed they were being subtle.

"Rick," she said gently, "Sullivan asked me to check in with you. He's worried."

Rick's shoulders tightened slightly.

"You've been carrying a lot," she continued. "The multicity tours. The talk shows appearances. Always moving. Always on. And I haven't once seen you really let your guard down."

She paused, watching him carefully.

"I've only known you since Thanksgiving," she added, "but I've been around long enough to recognize when someone is restless for a reason." Rick said nothing.

"And don't think I missed that little hallway argument you and Sullivan had yesterday," she said lightly. "You're not as quiet as you think."

Rick clenched the nutcracker a little tighter.

"We were just talking."

"Talking? Sure." She raised an eyebrow. "But you meant every word you said."

He didn't respond.

He didn't have to.

Brandy wiped her hands on a towel and came around to lean against the counter beside him. "I get it. You've spent years making sure Sullivan shines. You smooth things out, run interference, fix every detail before anyone else realizes it's broken. And you're good at it."

Rick cracked another pecan, slower this time. "He's, my friend. He's always looked out for me."

"And that matters," Brandy said softly. "But it doesn't mean you stay in his shadow."

Rick shifted, uncomfortable.

"You told him you want to write," she continued. "A screenplay. Not someday. Not hypothetically. You said it out loud."

"It's just an idea," Rick said.

"No," she said, touching the side of the bowl. "It's a direction."

He looked toward the window. Snow drifted like confetti, gentle, relentless. Christmas Eve in Wintercrest. A week until his New Year's Eve party back in New York. He should've been excited about the countdown, the energy, the crowd. Instead, something low in his chest tugged.

"Why do you think he doesn't believe you're ready?" Brandy asked, not unkindly.

Rick exhaled. "Because he's always seen me as the kid."

She waited.

"He had to be strict with me," Rick said. "Money. Women. The people I was hanging around. Even my career. I made some dumb choices back then. He stepped in when nobody else did."

"And now?" she pushed.

"And now he still thinks I need a green light before I move," Rick said quietly. "Like if he doesn't think I'm ready for that writers' room, I shouldn't be there at all."

Brandy nodded. "And what if he's wrong?"

Rick let out a short breath. "He's not wrong often."

"But he's not always right," she said plainly. "He's your guy. I get that. But if he doesn't see you as ready, that doesn't mean you aren't. It means you find another route. You show him. Or you don't. Either way, you stop waiting."

Rick huffed quietly and reached for another pecan. "You know I didn't sign up to be psychoanalyzed. I just wanted to help you bake a pie."

She smiled. "And yet, here you are."

He snorted. "If I'd known this came with career advice, I would've stayed in the living room."

"But you didn't," she said gently. "Because you're tired of pretending you don't want more."

Rick stared at the mixture in the bowl. That was too close. Too accurate.

"My life works better when it's simple," he said carefully.

Brandy smiled knowingly. "Except it's not simple now, is it?"

He shot her a warning look. "Don't start."

"Oh, I already did," she said, amused. "And I'm almost done."

She tapped the wooden spoon. "Go on. Stir."

He did, slow and steady, letting the warmth ease into his hands.

"Pecan pie takes patience," Brandy said quietly. "You can't rush it. You can't fake it. But when you trust yourself enough to follow it through, it holds."

Rick glanced at her. "That better not be another metaphor."

She smiled. "It absolutely is."

"And for what it's worth," she added, softer, "you're allowed to want something that isn't tied to someone else's approval."

Rick exhaled, long and quiet.

He didn't say Asha's name.

He didn't have to.

Her laugh drifted in from the living room, bright and unguarded, pulling his attention before he could stop himself.

Brandy noticed.

She said nothing.

As he poured the filling into the pie shell, the cabin filled with the scent of brown sugar and toasted pecans. Something warm. Something familiar. Something that felt like possibility. Rick was in trouble. And for the first time, he wasn't sure he wanted saving.

CHAPTER TWELVE

Wintercrest didn't believe in subtle Christmas. By the time Asha made it downstairs, the cabin was alive, warm, noisy, and glowing like it had been waiting all year for this moment. The bannisters were wrapped in twinkling lights, cinnamon and rosemary drifted out of the kitchen, and a soulful. Christmas playlist floated through the air, smooth enough to make even the storm outside feel gentle.

The dining table was already being set. Stockings hung unevenly. The fire crackled like it had opinions. And for the first time in a long while, Asha felt the ache of belonging. Soft. Foreign. Hopeful in a way that made her chest tight.

"ASHA!" Ryan's voice floated from the kitchen. "Do not just stand there looking adorable, come get some good shots of everyone cooking a dinner I absolutely did not cook.!"

Asha laughed under her breath and stepped into the whirlwind. Brandy was glazing the ham Ryan planned to brag about. Fabian was fussing over a centerpiece made of pinecones and cranberries. Desiree narrated everything like she was filming a holiday documentary.

Asha slipped between them, tucking napkins into place and adjusting silverware. It all felt... warm. Familiar, even though it shouldn't. This was Christmas Eve. And then her phone buzzed. She pulled it from her pocket out of habit, just a quick glance, hardly thinking and then she froze.

An email banner lit her screen:

NYE Branding Shoot–Confirming Availability
Client: Sirius Beatz, Platinum-Producing Artist
Her heart skipped twice.

The message preview below made her breath catch:

Can you fly out after Christmas day? Need you on set Dec 27 – Jan 1. Rate approved. Team excited.

Asha's knees nearly buckled. This wasn't just another brand job. This was *the* job. The one that cracked open doors that stayed locked for most people. She clicked the message open, devouring every line.

Her mind raced.

Chicago first.

Check on Grandma.

Swap bags.

Then New York.

A skyline.

A studio.

A New Year's Eve project that could change everything.

Her fingers were already swiping open an airline app before she could think twice. **Christmas red-eye flight to Chicago O'Hare: available.**

Her pulse thrummed with adrenaline.

She wasn't leaving tonight.

She wasn't abandoning the Winter Wonderland shoot she'd promised Ryan.

She just... needed a head start.

Christmas Eve was still hers to give.

She'd keep the magic going for everyone. Especially for Ryan.

Asha selected the flights.

Her thumb hovered over Purchase.

Footsteps approached.

She tapped out of the airline site so fast she nearly sprained her wrist.

Ryan leaned over her shoulder with the energy of a caffeinated elf. "Okay! What do you think for Christmas Eve? I'm thinking soft neutrals. Sparkly snow. Cozy-but-elegant hearth energy. Should we get shots with the mugs? I wanna give grown-woman Hallmark with just a touch of 'I own property.'"

Asha pasted on a smile. "Perfect. Come see the proofs from yesterday, the fireplace ones are insane."

"Oh, absolutely yes, show me!" Ryan squealed, all dimples and delight.

Asha flipped to her gallery, pretending her pulse wasn't still racing.

Ryan gasped dramatically. "OH! These! ASHA! You captured my soul in this one."

"Your soul is dramatic," Asha said, nudging her.

"Exactly." Ryan beamed. "Okay, tonight we do the full Winter Wonderland set. And tomorrow morning we swap gifts and do pajamas by the tree. I already coordinated colors."

Asha nodded, forcing her brain back into the moment. "We'll get everything. I promise."

Ryan bounced away, humming like she was floating.

Asha let out a shaky breath.

She wasn't hiding this opportunity.

Just... holding it close until the moment was right.

Tonight belonged to Ryan and her friends.

She wasn't ruining it with plans they didn't need to hear yet.

The living room filled as the evening rolled in. Jackson and Gabby were locked in playing chess in the den. Desiree and Marcus were out on the patio taking selfies and roasting marshmallows.

Brandy and Sullivan curled up near the fireplace, talking about life the way couples do when they believe love is a safe place.

Ryan and Fabian dragged Asha into an impromptu snow-white photo shoot by the tree, fussing with lighting and angles and the "perfect level of whimsy."

And in the center of it all stood Rick.

He wasn't participating-not fully, but he wasn't hiding either. He leaned against the back of the sofa, casual and composed, scrolling his phone with that quiet intensity he wore like armor. Firelight softened him, brushing warm shadows along his jaw, making him look almost... gentle.

Asha felt his stare before she saw it.

When she finally looked up, his eyes were already on her.

Not annoyed.

Not irritated.

Just... present.

A flicker of something neither of them had language for.

She glanced away quickly, suddenly too warm in her own skin.

Rick straightened, sliding his phone into his pocket like he hadn't been watching her for the last thirty seconds.

He didn't come over.

But he didn't leave the room either.

It was the oddest, softest tension that settled between them. Steady and undeniable beneath the holiday commotion.

Ryan waved a glittery ornament at Rick. "Hey! Rick! Smile!"

"I don't smile on command," Rick muttered.

Asha smirked. "He doesn't smile at all."

His eyes narrowed at her. "I smile when things make sense."

"Oh," she countered sweetly, "so never."

Brandy snorted. "Lord... the flirting is about to set this tree on fire."

Asha's mouth fell open. "Nobody is flirting!"

Rick's jaw ticked. "Definitely not."

But the air between them disagreed. Asha moved back toward the fireplace, wrapping her arms around herself. She needed a breath, a break, something to settle her racing thoughts, both about New York and the man trying extremely hard not to look at her again.

She noticed his reflection in the window. Hands in pockets. Shoulders relaxed. Expression unreadable. Except she could read it. He was fighting something too.

She turned away before she gave too much away in return. Christmas Eve at Wintercrest was loud, warm, and holiday magic swirled through every room.

But the most unsettling part of the night, the part she carried with her long after the laughter softened, was how often she noticed Rick looking her way...

...and how impossible it became to pretend she didn't feel something shift inside her every time he did.

Tomorrow meant presents, cocoa, and an immediate flight out of Wintercrest.

But tonight... tonight was lights and mistletoe and that quiet little feeling settling between them, steady and impossible to ignore.

CHAPTER THIRTEEN

The patio was wrapped in a layer of cold so clean and sharp it almost crackled in the air. Sullivan, Fabian, Marcus, and Rick stood in a loose circle, smoke curling from their cigars, the scent warm and earthy against the winter air.

Sullivan exhaled slowly, the tip of his cigar glowing. "Man, if y'all had seen me in undergrad..." He shook his head, laughing. "Broke. Hungry. Writing romance scenes in a freezing dorm room where the heat clicked on maybe twice a week. My roommate used to clown me for typing love monologues while wearing gloves."

Fabian choked on a laugh. "Not gloves."

"Oh yes," Sullivan said, raising his hand. "Fingerless. Because I needed to type."

Marcus slapped his knee. "Ain't no way. Not you out here giving Nicholas Sparks in a dorm with no heat."

Sullivan shrugged. "Look, when you want something badly enough, pride stops mattering. I was grinding. And Brandy-" His whole face softened. "She believed in me before anyone else did."

Marcus puffed his cigar, pulling in a slow drag like he was preparing for a sermon. "Look, let me tell y'all something about Desiree."

Rick leaned back, already anticipating foolishness.

Marcus continued, "I met that woman at a Fourth of July barbecue in Richmond. She had on these blue jeans-Lord have mercy-and a white tank top, hair in a puff. She walked past me once. Didn't look at me. Not a glance. I said okay... maybe she ain't see me."

Fabian snorted. "She saw you."

"Oh, she absolutely saw me," Marcus agreed. "Next time she walked by, I tried again. Said, 'Excuse me, miss, can I talk to you for a second?'

She said," he slipped into Desiree's voice, slightly higher and full of attitude

"Talk to me for what?"

Sullivan doubled over laughing. "That sounds exactly like her."

Marcus pointed his cigar at them like it was evidence. "That girl curved me four months in a row. I mean, I was showing up to events I had no business at. Baby showers. Church cookouts. A lash install class."

Fabian wheezed. "You learned how to do lashes for a woman?"

"Damn right!" Marcus laughed. "Now she got me at the glam bar taking clients man" They all howled in laughter.

Rick smirked despite himself. "So, what changed?"

Marcus grinned slow. "She told me later she knew I wasn't interested in learning how to do lashes. Said she was waiting to see if I was consistent. If I actually liked her or just liked the chase." He shrugged. "I passed the test. Been stuck with her ever since."

Fabian raised his cigar. "Now that is love."

Marcus nodded. "That's work. Real work. But worth it."

Fabian leaned against the railing, blowing smoke into the cold air. "Man, Ryan almost left me after two weeks because I forgot our 'anniversary.'"

Rick blinked. "Two weeks? Why would she,"

"That's what I said!" Fabian threw his hands up. "Apparently Ryan counts time in emotions, not days. She was like, 'Baby, you didn't remember the anniversary of when you made me tea in your favorite mug.' I said, Ryan... that was Tuesday."

Sullivan laughed so hard he lost the ash from his cigar. "Did you apologize?"

"Oh, I apologized like my life depended on it," Fabian said. "I brought flowers. Chocolates. A playlist. I took her to brunch. You know Ryan-dramatic. But she forgave me after she realized I didn't have the emotional bandwidth to memorize romantic timestamps."

Rick found himself laughing along with them, feeling something loosen in his chest. The cigar didn't warm him as much as the camaraderie did. The shared stories, the messy vulnerability, the fact that these men had lived enough love to offer advice without condescension.

Marcus tapped the ash off his cigar and said, "Let me tell you something, Rick. When a woman gets under your skin like that? When she interrupts your peace but somehow makes the interruption feel like a good thing? Don't run from that."

Rick tensed, pulse flickering at the edges.

Fabian chimed in, softer now, "The good ones don't always come quiet. Sometimes they come loud. Sometimes they drag you into growth. Sometimes they annoy the hell out of you. Doesn't mean they're not meant to be in your life."

Sullivan nodded, giving Rick a steady look. "You don't have to figure it all out tonight, man. But don't close a door just because you're scared of what's behind it."

Rick looked away, heart thudding harder than he wanted it to. He had come outside for air, for space and they'd accidentally given him more truth than oxygen.

He cleared his throat. "I'm gonna check on something inside."

Sullivan smirked knowingly. "Yeah. Go do that."

Inside the cabin, the air changed instantly. It was warmer, softer, and quieter. He stepped into the living room... and stopped walking altogether.

She was there.

Asha stood on her toes at the base of the Christmas tree, frowning up at a stubborn strand of lights that refused to shine. The tree towered over her, shimmering everywhere except for one dark, irritating patch. Her red Christmas sweater hugged her frame, her jeans tucked into fuzzy red socks, and her short curls held the golden light in a way that made his breath shorten without warning.

She muttered something under her breath, gently shaking the strand like she could intimidate it into cooperation.

Rick leaned against the doorway with a soft huff. "You planning to fight the lights into submission?"

She gasped and spun around. "Can you not sneak up on people? Some of us have nerves."

He shrugged. "Some of us know how electricity works."

Asha narrowed her eyes. "Oh, you're an electrician now?"

"Move."

"No."

"Asha..."

She sighed dramatically and stepped aside, sweeping her hand toward the tree. "Fine. Impress me."

He crouched near the outlet, traced the line of wires, and found the tiny loose connector near the base. One small twist-

The tree burst into warm golden light.

Asha blinked, stunned by the glow. "Show-off."

But her voice softened around the edges, warm and appreciative in a way that tugged at him.

He stood again, the glow from the tree washing over them. For a moment, the room felt suspended, the fire crackling, snow pattering softly against the windows, the tree casting a halo of light across her face and glasses.

She looked... beautiful.

Unexpectedly beautiful.

"Thanks," she murmured. "I needed this shot before we start the gift exchange. Ryan will cry if I don't."

"I figured."

She looked up at him then, her eyes lingering longer than they should have. "Hey... about earlier. With Sullivan. I didn't want him brushing you off. You deserved to be heard."

His throat tightened. "Thank you. It meant more than you think."

"Same goes for the diner. The drive. The disaster of it all. You didn't have to deal with me losing my mind in a snowstorm."

"Trust me," he said quietly, "I've dealt with worse."

But something about the way she softened and the way her eyes warmed as she looked at him, made the joke feel smaller than the moment deserved.

The space between them changed.

Grew.

Shifted.

Asha stepped a little closer, almost without noticing. Rick held his breath a bit because... God. He felt it. The spark. The pull. The sharp, aching awareness of how close she was and how easily he could reach out and touch her.

"Hand me one of those bulbs," she said softly, nodding toward the box near the archway.

He walked over, kneeling beside it unaware of the mistletoe dangling above him.

He picked up a bulb.

Wrong one.

Asha came over to grab the right one, and they both leaned in at the same time, their heads bumping gently as they looked inside the box.

"Ouch! Watch it," she whispered, laughing under her breath.

"Maybe don't hover," he muttered, but he was smiling too.

They both stood at once...

And froze.

Together, they looked up.

Right above them hung a small, cheap mistletoe, plastic berries and ribbon swinging from the archway.

Asha's lips parted, her eyes widening just slightly. "Well," she whispered, her voice a warm little dare, "I guess I gotta let you kiss me, Franklin."

He swallowed. Hard. "Only if you actually want me to."

The air tightened. It was warm, trembling, and electric. His heartbeat thudded somewhere in his throat. She stepped closer, fingertips brushing his sleeve.

It was enough to undo him. The room blurred. The tree glowed. Her breathing mixed with his. They leaned in...just a little, just enough that everything in him reached for her. Just enough that her breath touched his.

Just enough that the entire moment felt like it could rewrite everything between them. And then The patio door slid open. Voices flooded in, loud and oblivious. Fabian laughed about something Marcus said. Sullivan followed behind them, and while the other guys didn't notice a thing, Sullivan caught one look at Rick's face-then one at Asha's.

He smirked. "Rick! Remember what we talked about," he said, clapping his shoulder on his way inside.

Asha jumped back, clutching the bulb like it was evidence of a crime. Rick pretended to dig through the box like the world's most stressed electrician.

The men walked past them, none the wiser.

But Sullivan?

He knew.

And Rick knew that he knew.

Asha hurried back to the tree, fixing the bulb with shaky hands. Rick kept his eyes on the box, trying to slow the pounding in his chest.

When she finally glanced his way again, their eyes met, shy, startled, and mixed with something neither of them was ready to name.

The almost-kiss still hung between them.

Hot. Tempting. And very, very real.

CHAPTER FOURTEEN

Asha clutched the spare bulb in her hand like it was an anchor to keep her from floating away. Her pulse was still fluttering-when she spotted Ryan near the cocoa bar, fussing with marshmallows shaped like tiny snowflakes.

Asha inhaled deeply, collected herself, then crossed the room.

"Ry?" Asha said softly. "Can I steal you for a sec?"

Ryan glanced up immediately, sensing something in her tone. "Yeah, of course. Come on." She tugged Asha toward a quiet corner near the hallway, away from the noise, away from the men's voices and the lingering hum of mistletoe energy Asha could still feel on her skin.

Ryan folded her arms, concern warming her expression. "What's going on? You look like you're holding your breath."

Asha exhaled. "Okay... don't freak out."

Ryan's eyes widened. "Girl, that is literally the worst way to start a sentence."

Asha laughed under her breath, a shaky, nervous sound, then said, "I'm leaving tomorrow."

Ryan blinked. "Tomorrow morning? As in... after gift exchange?"

"No, no. much later," Asha shook her head. "I booked a red-eye flight to Chicago."

Ryan's voice softened. "A red eye? Is your grandma okay?"

"She's fine," Asha said quickly. "I just have to get back fast and check in with her before I..." She hesitated. "Before I go to New York."

Ryan's brows shot up. "New York?"

Asha swallowed. "I got the branding gig with Sirius Beatz team."

Ryan's jaw dropped. "THEE Sirius Beatz? Mega-producer, diamond plaques, stadium tours-that Sirius Beatz?"

Asha nodded again.

Ryan let out a little gasp and grabbed both of Asha's hands. "ASHA! Oh my God! Why didn't you lead with THAT? That is huge!"

Asha smiled, overwhelmed. "I know. I just... I wanted tonight to be about your Christmas Eve shoot. And I didn't want you to think I was bailing sooner than agreed."

Ryan rolled her eyes, touched. "Girl, please. You could've told me in the middle of the photo shoot and I would've paused everything to celebrate with you."

Asha's voice softened. "Everything for tomorrow is already prepped. The photo plan, the edits, the content outline. I'll send everything over to you by Friday at the latest."

Ryan squeezed her hands. "Asha... congratulations. Seriously. This is massive. I am so, so proud of you."

Before Asha could reply, Brandy walked over, holding two mugs of cocoa. "What are we celebrating?"

Ryan smiled. "Our girl here is about to pack her bags for New York. She will be working with a mega star."

Brandy's face lit up. "Oh, girl, come here." She set the mugs down and pulled Asha into a tight hug. "See? I told you things were turning around. All that hard work, it's paying off."

Asha felt her throat tighten. "I hope so."

Brandy cupped her cheek gently. "No hoping. Believe it. You deserve every good thing coming your way."

Ryan nodded. "Exactly. And don't worry about us. We'll be fine. You go handle your business. You've given me such a great winter wonderland for a lifetime."

They both smiled at her, their support settling beneath her ribs, steady, grounding, and real.

But when Asha stepped away...

Her thoughts drifted back to the living room.

Back to the Christmas tree lights.

Back to the mistletoe hanging over her head.

Back to Rick standing a little too close, breathing a little too softly, looking at her like maybe everything between them was shifting.

She swallowed hard.

Because in the rush of good news and flights and deadlines...

His face kept rising in her mind.

What if there could be something there?

What if timing ruins it before it even starts?

And does she even have room in her life for something like this?

Asha forced herself to rejoin the noise of the cabin, smiling, nodding, and accepting another mug of cocoa from Ryan.

But Rick stayed in her head.

Warm.

Unexpected.

Hard to shake in the most alluring way.

And the way he'd looked at her under that mistletoe...

It wasn't going anywhere.

IT WAS WELL PAST MIDNIGHT when Asha finally gave up on sleep.

Her body was exhausted, but her mind?

Her mind was somewhere else entirely.

Her mind was replaying one thing on a loop:

Rick.

Rick under the mistletoe.

Rick looking at her like the whole world had gone silent.

Rick leaning in slow, careful... like she was something fragile and important.

Rick pulling back at the exact second she wanted him not to.

She breathed in sharply, the memory hitting her like a warm rush across her chest. It wasn't just the almost-kiss.

It was the way his body had felt standing close to hers, solid, warm, broad shoulders and steady hands. A man who took up space without trying, the sort of man you noticed even when you pretended you didn't. She could still feel the heat of him, the way his cologne lingered in the air between them, the way her breath had shifted because... God, he was sexy.

Not cute.

Not handsome in that polite way.

Sexy.

She groaned into her pillow. Nope. Not doing this. Not thinking about his deep brown eyes or how her breath had gotten stuck in her throat or how close their mouths had been.

She remembered the first day they met, how grumpy he'd been, how annoyingly rigid he was, how she was absolutely convinced she would despise him for the entire trip. And now here she was... thinking about the curve of his jaw, the heat in his eyes, the way his voice dipped low when he said her name.

"Nope," she whispered, throwing back her blanket.

If she wasn't going to sleep, she was at least going to eat.

She padded quietly down the stairs, the cabin dark except for the soft glow of the fireplace embers. Her socks whispered against the hardwood floor as she stepped into the kitchen.

And there it was.

On a plate.

Wrapped in plastic.

Waiting for her like a divine Christmas miracle.

The last slice of Brandy's pecan pie.

Asha folded her hands dramatically. "Thank you, Lord. You see your child."

She reached for the plate,

A low voice murmured behind her.

"Don't tell me you're about to steal the last slice."

She jumped, hand flying to her chest. "Can you not sneak around like a serial killer?"

Rick stood in the doorway, wearing gray sweats and a white tee, messy hair, eyes heavy with sleep, looking annoyingly good for someone who was supposed to be her mortal enemy.

His focus flicked to the pie. "I came down here for that."

Asha pulled the plate closer. "Well, I found it first."

He stepped into the kitchen, slow, deliberate. "I've had a long day."

"Same."

"I think I deserve it more."

She scoffed. "Boy, please. I got stranded with you. That alone earns me dessert rights."

He tilted his head, fighting a smile. "We can solve this the mature way, you know."

"Oh? And what way is that?"

He reached into the drawer, grabbed two forks, and set them beside the plate.

"One slice," he said softly. "Two forks."

The air shifted, softening, warming, and bending toward something she didn't want to name out loud.

But she nodded.

"Fine," she murmured.

They sat at the kitchen island, shoulders brushing every so often, pretending not to notice how close they were. The cabin around them was silent, wrapped in snow and moonlight.

Rick took the first bite, humming under his breath. Asha rolled her eyes.

"Don't act like Brandy didn't snap her fingers at you to help make it."

"It's good," he said. "And I'm allowed to enjoy things."

"Wow. Growth."

He nudged her shoulder lightly. "Your turn."

She took a bite.

Sweet. Warm. Perfect.

Everything the moment shouldn't be... and yet was. They fell into a quiet rhythm-fork, laugh, soft joke, fork again. And then it happened. She reached for a piece at the same time he did. Their fingers brushed. Not a casual brush. Not an accidental tap.

A slow, lingering glide of warmth against warmth. Asha froze. He did too. Her eyes lifted first. His followed. The air between them tightened, thickened, heated in a way that had nothing to do with pie or cocoa or Christmas lights. Her breath stuttered. His lips parted slightly like he was thinking the same thing as she was: Don't move. Don't breathe. Don't break this moment. He leaned in an inch. She leaned in two. By the time their foreheads almost touched, the decision had already been made.

The kiss came softly at first.

A shy press of warm lips, cautious, curious, almost questioning. Then deeper, sweeter, fuller-like the taste of sweet roasted pecans melting against heat. Her hand slid to his jaw. His fingers brushed her waist. The world tilted, gently, beautifully.

When they finally pulled apart, their breaths mingled in a trembling space between them.

Rick swallowed. "Asha..."

She shook her head quickly, pulse thundering. "Don't. Please don't say anything yet." Because she didn't trust her heart. Because she didn't trust the way she wanted to lean right back in. Because everything about this man-this moment...felt too big and too fragile to name.

All she could admit was the truth humming inside her: This wasn't supposed to happen. Not with her life shifting again. Not with New York calling and her career finally cracking open new doors.

Not with everything she'd worked for finally beginning to take shape. Wanting him felt risky. Like choosing him might complicate everything she'd spent the year trying to rebuild. But she didn't want it to stop. Not now. Not ever.

CHAPTER FIFTEEN

Christmas morning should have felt soft and familiar, a gentle quiet Rick remembered from childhood visits to his aunt's house in Georgia. The sound of people waking slowly and happily.

Instead, Rick woke with the imprint of Asha's lips still lingering on his skin. That sweet, unexpected pecan pie kiss. The warmth of her body pressed into his beneath the mistletoe. The way she had fit against him like it had always been meant to happen that way.

He wanted her.

He wanted her in a way that felt reckless. Like stepping into a risk, he had no business taking.

Sleep had been impossible. His body felt wired, restless, and every nerve pulled tight. He dressed quietly, needing space before he did something he could not take back. The cabin was still dim, Christmas lights humming softly along the living room wall. Cinnamon and nutmeg drifted faintly through the vents. Brandy, most likely.

Rick stepped into the hallway just as he heard Asha's voice.

Low. Warm. A little frayed around the edges, like she had slept just as badly as he had.

She was in the small office nook off the living room, pacing slowly, phone pressed to her ear. He had not meant to listen. He never meant to listen. But when he heard the word "New York," he stopped.

"I'm honored," she said, her voice soft but strained. "Really. It's an unbelievable opportunity. I just don't know if I can commit to being in New York for anything longer. Can we go over the details when I get there for the shoot?"

She continued, quieter now. "I already booked a flight home to Chicago today. I need to check in with my grandma. I haven't told her about this yet, and I promised I would always talk to her before starting anything new. She's all I have, and I'm all she has. Then I'll head to New York. He needs me there the day after tomorrow, right?"

Rick stilled.

Already booked.

His chest tightened, not because of the distance, but because the decision had already been made. Because the kiss had not slowed her down.

The words echoed louder than anything else she said.

"I'm actually ready to leave Wintercrest," she said, her voice quieter now. "I have cabin fever bad, being cooped up in here."

Leaving Wintercrest. Leaving the cabin so soon. Leaving before he could figure out what last night meant.

A pause followed.

Rick heard the faint sound of a woman's voice on the other end of the line. Calm. Reassuring. A soft chuckle drifting through the doorway.

"I understand," the woman said. "Let's put a pin in it until you get here. We'll talk it through."

Asha exhaled. "Thank you. I appreciate that."

Rick closed his eyes.

He had let himself believe the kiss meant intention. She had kept it moving. He knew better. He knew she was talking about responsibility. Family. A future she was afraid to reach for too fast. He admired that. Respected it. But it still stung. She had not told him. Some foolish part of him had hoped the kiss meant she might want to talk. About what came next. About possibility. About timing.

Instead, he was learning she was leaving through a doorway he had never meant to stand behind.

Rick backed away quietly. His heel brushed the wall.

Inside the office, Asha paused.

"Hello?" she called out.

Rick did not answer.

He slipped down the hall, the warmth of the cabin suddenly thinner than it had been moments before.

SOON AFTER

Christmas morning came alive in the softest way. Pajamas. Coffee. Laughter drifting from the kitchen. The fire crackled low. Someone hummed along to an old Christmas playlist.

Rick noticed all of it, even as his chest stayed tight.

He kept himself busy so he would not think too hard. He made coffee. Straightened throw blankets. Packed his things. He wiped down a counter that did not need wiping.

Sullivan sat on the arm of the sofa, scrolling through his phone.

Rick walked over, grateful for something normal.

"Morning," he said.

"Morning," Sullivan replied. "Roads reopened. Flights should be back on schedule by midday."

"That's good," Rick said. "I'm planning to head back to New York on the next available flight. Need to salvage what's left of my break. Tighten up plans for my New Year's Eve party. I've had enough of this place. I need to move around."

Sullivan nodded slowly. "Yeah. I know how much that party means to you."

Rick's mouth tipped into a small smile. "You do?"

"Of course I do," Sullivan said. "You don't half-step anything you care about."

Rick took a sip of coffee, letting the warmth settle him.

Sullivan glanced at his phone again, then back up. "Actually... I've been thinking more about that conversation we had. About you wanting to get your feet wet with screenwriting."

Rick stilled. Just slightly.

"I reached out to Jerry," Sullivan continued, casual like it wasn't a big deal. "He's EP'ing that project we talked about. Asked if he might need another set of hands in the writers' room. He said to have you hit him up after New Year's."

Rick's phone buzzed. "Check your phone, I just sent you his contact."

Rick stared at his screen for a beat longer than necessary.

"You didn't have to do that," he said quietly.

Sullivan shrugged. "Yeah, I did. You're ready. And you've been ready."

Gratitude hit first. And then the quiet realization that if Asha hadn't spoken up for him the way she had, if she hadn't seen him the way she did, maybe Sullivan would not have made the call at all.

"Thank you," Rick said.

Sullivan smiled. "We'll talk details after the holidays. For now, go do your thing."

Rick nodded.

Behind him, footsteps moved quickly down the stairs.

"Ayeee, Merry Christmas," Asha said brightly. "Why does it smell so good in here already?"

She sounded like herself. Light. Warm. Awake.

Rick did not turn around right away.

She moved through the room easily, bumping Brandy's shoulder, laughing at something Fabian said, asking about cinnamon rolls like she had not cracked something open in Rick's chest an hour earlier.

"Rick," she said when she finally noticed him. "Did you sleep at all?"

He nodded once. "A little."

"That makes one of us," she said with a soft laugh. "I feel like I've been up all night."

She smiled at him.

The same smile from last night.

Rick looked away.

Something in him tightened, quiet and defensive.

Asha kept moving, still warm in a way that made the distance between them feel sharper. She talked. She laughed. She floated through the space like nothing had shifted at all.

Rick stayed where he was.

When she drifted closer, he stepped back. When she spoke to him, he answered politely. Briefly.

When she brushed past him, he did not let himself lean in. He told himself it was self-preservation. He told himself he was giving her space. But the truth was simpler and uglier. He was hurt.

He replayed everything in his head. Her voice on the phone. Her talk of leaving. His words to Sullivan about going back to New York. Had he misread everything? This was probably nothing but a good time for her. A moment she could step into and out of without consequence.

Rick swallowed hard.

He hated how quickly his mind went there, how easily doubt filled in the gaps she had never meant to leave. How fast he started to feel like a stop along the way instead of someone she might have chosen.

The thought sat heavy in his chest. Rick wanted something that he couldn't control, and he wanted it anyway.

CHAPTER SIXTEEN

Asha came down the stairs still riding the thin edge of adrenaline and had no sleep. Her body felt wired. Thoughts scattered. Christmas morning energy buzzing through her veins, even though something underneath it felt... off.

She heard Rick's voice before she saw him.

Low. Controlled. Too even.

"...next available flight back to New York," he was saying. "I need to tighten things up for New Year's Eve."

She slowed halfway down the stairs.

Sullivan answered easily, familiar. "Yeah. I know how much that party means to you."

Asha's fingers tightened around the stair rail.

New York.

Flights.

Leaving.

Rick's voice again. "I've had enough of this place. I need to move around."

The words landed sharper than she expected.

She told herself not to read into it. Not to assume anything. But the timing felt cruel. Too close to the moment they had shared. Too close to the way his mouth had lingered like it meant something.

She forced her feet to keep moving.

By the time she hit the bottom step, her smile was already in place.

"Ayeee, Merry Christmas," she said brightly. "Why does it smell so good in here already?"

Rick didn't turn around right away.

That stung more than it should have.

She moved through the room anyway, momentum carrying her forward. Every attempt to talk to him met a short reply, clipped and polite, like he didn't care to linger. No teasing. No softness. No trace of the man who had kissed her the night before.

Something in her chest dipped. Not enough to show. Just enough to notice. She told herself not to be ridiculous. They hadn't promised each other anything. This wasn't a love story. It was a few days. A cabin. A kiss that maybe meant more to her than it ever had to him.

Still, doubt crept in. Had she imagined the weight of it? Had she mistaken proximity for intention? She kept moving. She always did.

But as she crossed the room to start setting up her equipment, the warmth she usually carried felt thinner. More deliberate. Like she was holding it in place instead of letting it spill naturally.

She adjusted the tripod, checked her lens, and moved through the living room like muscle memory had taken over. Lights were strung just right. Ornaments caught the glow. Gift boxes were stacked neatly near the fireplace, ready for the final set of photos Ryan wanted.

Rick stood near the window.

Arms crossed. Phone in hand. Scrolling like there was something more important happening on that screen than in the room.

She walked over and bumped his arm lightly with hers, the way she had done all week. Familiar. Easy.

"So, Franklin," she murmured, keeping her voice low so only he could hear, "are you going to keep pretending we did not kiss last night, or should I schedule that conversation for after lunch?"

Rick did not look up.

"It was just a kiss," he said. "Nothing special."

The words hit harder than she expected.

Before she could stop herself, Asha snatched the phone from his hand.

Rick finally looked at her.

They stood there, staring at each other. Asha searched his face for something. Anything. A sign that she had not imagined the way he kissed her. Rick's expression was closed off, unreadable.

A few heads turned.

Fabian raised his eyebrows. "Y'all good over there?"

Rick reached out, took his phone back from her grip, and slipped it into his pocket.

"It does not matter," he said quietly. "You already booked your flight."

He met her eyes then, something guarded settling into his expression.

"I just wish I had known what this was to you."

The words landed wrong.

Asha blinked. "What?"

"You are leaving," he continued, his voice flat. "And clearly this was just some holiday fun for you. Seems like you have it all figured out."

Asha's mouth parted, heat rushing up her neck.

"That's funny," she said, too quick, too sharp. "Because from where I was standing, you were the one already planning your exit."

Rick's jaw tightened.

He didn't respond.

He just stepped away.

Just like that.

He walked past her, already looking for an exit.

The space he left behind felt louder than anything he could have said.

Heat crawled up Asha's neck. Embarrassment. Confusion. Hurt, all tangled together.

"Nah, we good," she said quickly, answering Fabian's question, forcing a laugh that sounded fake. "I forgot the Grinch still celebrates Christmas in his own way."

Desiree let out a soft laugh. "Well damn. And just when I thought we were getting a happily ever after."

Asha cut her eyes toward Desiree but couldn't help the smile that slipped out anyway. It was what she did when she refused to be embarrassed.

"Aye, chill," she said lightly, lifting her camera. "Some of us are here to work."

She threw herself back into the shoot.

She directed Fabian and Ryan through gift exchanges. Adjusted angles. Asked Desiree, Gabby, Brandy, and Ryan to pose together, laughing like they were in the middle of a Waiting to Exhale scene. She added extra shots. Hands passing wrapped boxes. Close-ups of smiles. Ornaments clinking together.

She delivered exactly what Ryan needed. By midday, she was exhausted. And ready to leave. That was the moment something in her closed.

She broke down her setup quickly. Camera packed. Lenses secured. Tripod folded. She slung the bag over her shoulder and headed upstairs without announcing it. Only then did packing begin.

She stood in the middle of the guest room with her suitcase open on the bed, stuffing sweaters and socks into places they did not fit. She was upset, and she took it out on her luggage.

She replayed the morning on a loop. His voice: *You already booked your flight. Seems like you have it all figured out.*

She wanted to confront him. Clear the air. Say something. But she had seen him retreat out back with Sullivan, and the moment felt gone. Like the damage had already settled. Maybe that was all the kiss had been to him. A moment over pecan pie. A lapse in judgment. Her jaw tightened.

She balled up another sweater and shoved it into the suitcase.

"Men like that do not change overnight," she muttered.

Still, thoughts of him flooded her mind.

Rick laughing under the Christmas lights.

Rick's breath brushing her mouth beneath the mistletoe.

The certainty in the way he kissed her, like he had decided something.

Her chest tightened.

It would have been easier if he had stayed his rude, grumpy self the entire time.

She shoved her camera charger into a side pocket and swallowed the lump rising in her throat.

"Nope," she whispered, pressing a palm against her sternum. "We are not crying over a man we do not even know."

Except she did know him. More than she wanted. And that was the problem.

ASHA TUGGED ON HER airport outfit like armor.

Coffee-brown sweatsuit.

Matching puffer coat.

Timberland boots.

Soft gloss. Fresh, short curls styled and fluffy beneath her hat. She checked herself in the mirror.

Unbothered.

Fine.

Untouched by a man and his inconsistent behavior. She looked good enough to believe it for about five seconds. Then the truth crept in anyway. She was bothered. More than she had any right to be. And she hated that Rick had that kind of power without even trying.

BY THE TIME ASHA ROLLED her suitcases down the stairs, the cabin buzzed with that familiar end-of-holiday energy. People lingering. Stealing final moments of warmth before returning to real life.

Jackson leaned over the upstairs railing.

"Yo, Chi-town. Bring me back that caramel-cheese popcorn mix."

Asha laughed, pressing a hand to her chest. "I got you."

Desiree met her at the bottom of the stairs and pulled her into a hug so tight it knocked the air out of her.

"Girl, listen," Dez said into her ear. "Do not overthink men. They are slow. Like dial-up Internet slow."

Asha snorted. "Not dial-up."

"You heard me. Safe flight."

Brandy was next. Warm smile. Big-sister energy.

"You're stepping into something new," she whispered, rubbing Asha's arm. "Let it happen."

Asha nodded, even though her chest felt too full to speak.

Then Ryan barreled toward her like Asha was about to ship off to basic training.

"TEXT. ME. WHEN. YOU. LAND," she said, gripping both of Asha's hands. "And do not argue with TSA. I am serious."

Asha gave a weak laugh. "I'll be good."

"You won't," Ryan said. "But I'll pray."

Everyone laughed.

Everyone hugged her.

Everyone sent her off with love.

Everyone except the one person she kept looking for.

She scanned the living room.

Empty.

The kitchen.

Empty.

The back patio.

Empty.

Her stomach dropped.

His coat was gone.

His suitcase too.

She hesitated, then cracked open the door to his bedroom.

Her heart skipped.

The room looked untouched.

Bed made.

Lights off.

No sign he had ever been there.

Like he had vanished.

Like he had left before sunrise.

Before she could even try to understand last night.

Before she could make sense of the way he spoke to her that morning.

Before she could ask him what the kiss meant.

Before she could tell him she would be in Chicago for a day. Then New York. And maybe—

Maybe they could try something real.

Her throat tightened painfully.

"Wow," she whispered into the empty room. "Okay."

The thoughts spiraled fast.

Was he in a relationship?

Was everything a fluke?

Had she misread every look, every moment, every breath between them?

Why did she let herself want something?

"Girl," she muttered, swallowing hard, "you are a fool to think you could really talk sense into this man."

She shut the door with a shaky exhale.

HER UBER PULLED UP just as soft snow drifted across the driveway. Night had settled fully around the cabin, its windows glowing warm behind her, the kind of light that made everything inside feel safe and soft.

It hurt to leave it.

It hurt more that she was leaving without a goodbye from Rick.

As she slid into the back seat, buckling her coat closer around her, she whispered into the cold air:

"A few days shouldn't hurt like this."

But they did.

Oh, they did.

CHAPTER SEVENTEEN

B y the time Asha reached the jet bridge, she was already exhausted. The airport was peak holiday madness; cranky travelers arguing with gate agents, a toddler wailing like his spirit was leaving his body, overhead bins already full before anyone stepped on the plane. Snow whipped sideways across the terminal windows, and every few minutes a loudspeaker blared with another delay warning.

Perfect.

Just perfect.

She scanned her boarding pass again, mostly to distract herself from the dull ache behind her ribs.

Row 14. Seat B.

Middle seat.

Because God had jokes.

She stepped onto the plane second-to-last. Every row she passed felt tighter, warmer, louder. A flight attendant was fighting with a carry-on that refused to fit. Someone in row nine was coughing too dramatically to be real. The entire aircraft smelled like peppermint hand sanitizer and stress.

She clutched her tote, breathed out slowly, and prepared to squeeze herself into whatever stranger-filled situation awaited her.

Then she looked up. And her heart dropped straight to her boots. There he was. Rick. In Row 14. Head back against the seat. Hoodie up. Headphones in. A book resting open on his chest, his hand splayed across the page. He looked unfairly fine for someone who had ruined her sense of emotional stability. A rough shadow of stubble. Tired eyes. Broad shoulders straining against the hoodie in a way that made her pulse trip.

For a second, Asha thought her brain was playing games with her. Holiday delusion. Sleep deprivation. Wishful thinking. But no. He was right there. She froze in the aisle, staring like a complete idiot. Then she remembered to breathe and checked her boarding pass again.

Row 14.

Seat B.

Her seat.

"You've got to be kidding me," she whispered under her breath.

A man behind her cleared his throat pointedly, nudging her forward.

Asha swallowed her pride, lifted her chin, and gently stepped into the row, sliding into the middle seat. Their shoulders brushed. Warm. Solid. Immediate. Rick's eyes opened. Slowly. Like a man waking from a dream. He blinked once. Twice.

And then his expression shifted into something she couldn't quite name—shock, relief, disbelief, hope.

"You're kidding," he murmured.

Asha exhaled a shaky laugh. "Trust me... I'm as confused as you are."

He lifted one eyebrow. "This flight goes to Chicago."

She shot back, "I'm aware. What exactly are you doing on it?"

A slow, crooked smirk curved across his mouth. It caught her off guard, daring her to say something smart back.

"Heard there's a fine shawty out there."

She elbowed him lightly. "Boy, please."

But she was smiling. More than she had since she left the cabin.

THE CABIN LIGHTS DIMMED once everyone settled in. A baby cried somewhere near the front, turbulence rumbled beneath the plane, and snow streaked past the small oval windows like hurried brushstrokes.

Asha folded her hands in her lap, trying to slow her racing heart.

Rick sat rigid beside her, pretending to reread the same sentence in his book even though he clearly was not. After a moment, he turned toward her. Not rushed. Not nervous. Just steady.

Like he had finally decided to stop running from the thing that scared him most.

His voice was low. Warm. Honest.

"I haven't stopped thinking about that kiss," he said. "Or you."

"I just didn't know how to say any of it without messing everything up," he continued. "But I got some good advice. And it came down to this... I need to be where you are. If you want me there."

Asha stared at him, her heartbeat loud in her ears.

"Then why did you act like you couldn't wait to leave?" she asked quietly. "You looked... done. With me. With everything."

Rick winced, just a little. "Because feelings make me stupid...you make me stupid."

She blinked, caught between laughing and crying.

"I overheard your conversation earlier," he said. "And I jumped to conclusions. I got scared. And yeah... I felt foolish for even thinking a woman like you would slow down for me."

Asha shook her head. "If you hadn't been so nosy and gave me a chance, I would have told you everything. Things were just happening fast. And I wanted the moment to stay exactly where it was."

He lifted an eyebrow. "If I remember correctly, I wasn't the only one eavesdropping."

She laughed softly. "Yeah, but it sounded like you had good news."

He smiled. "Turns out we both did."

"And instead of talking about it," she said, teasing now, "we just—"

"Went a little crazy in that cabin," he finished.

"Just a little," she whispered, rolling her eyes.

"But I wasn't planning to let you go that easy," he added.

She scoffed. "Let me go."

Her shoulders finally relaxed. Something tight inside her loosened. Their hands brushed on the armrest. Light at first. Then intentional. His thumb traced her knuckles, careful and sincere. She did not pull away.

"You're weird," she whispered.

"I know."

"I like it," she said softly. "I like you."

The plane slipped into a smooth pocket of air as the seatbelt sign chimed off. Overhead lights flickered. The cabin settled.

Asha turned toward him.

He leaned in slowly, giving her time to change her mind. She did not. Their lips met in a soft, lingering kiss. No rush. No fireworks. Just warmth. Breath. Promise.

When they pulled apart, they exhaled at the same time.

"This should be fun," he murmured.

She smiled. Outside, the snow clouds thinned as the plane pressed on toward Chicago.

Inside Row 14, something real finally began.

CHAPTER EIGHTEEN

The plane touched down with a soft thud, and Rick felt it in his chest before he felt it under his feet. Chicago came into view through the window, all gray sky and light flurries drifting across the runway. It looked exactly like he remembered. Cold. Familiar. Steady.

But this time, something about it felt warmer. And that warmth had nothing to do with the city.

Asha stood a few rows ahead of him in the aisle, adjusting her brown puffer and smoothing a hand down the nape of her neck like she always did when she was settling herself. Rick followed close behind, not crowding her, but close enough that she could feel his presence. Close enough that he could tell she kept checking the corner of her eye for him.

He grabbed her carry-on from the overhead without thinking. It felt natural, like something he had done a hundred times already.

"Thanks," she said, a little breathless.

"Of course," he replied easily, even though his heart was still working overtime.

He had been to Chicago plenty of times. Touring with Sullivan. Passing through. Sleeping in hotels that all blurred together. But this trip was different.

This time, he was here on purpose. They walked through O'Hare in that quiet, unspoken way two people walked when they were still figuring each other out. Not awkward. Just careful. Like neither of them wanted to rush the shape of whatever this was becoming.

OUTSIDE, THE COLD HIT hard, sharp and immediate.

"You good?" he asked when she pulled her scarf tighter.

"I'm fine. This is home," she said, smiling softly.

Rick nodded. He understood more than she meant.

An Uber black SUV pulled up, and Rick opened the door for her before sliding in on the other side. He noticed the way she hesitated for half a second before sitting, like she was clocking how easy it all felt. That realization made her nervous.

It made him nervous too.

He leaned back against the seat. "What's the plan?"

"Well, I need to let my grandma know about the gig in New York. I'd rather tell her face to face plus we have this thing where no matter what, I check in with her. My Dad died when I was young and I never knew my mother. It's been me and her. "She said settling into her seat.

They had never spoken about parents or even the bond between her and her grandma. But he knew she meant the world to her, and he was even more infatuated with her.

She continued not missing a beat or noticing how he looked at her "Then pack for New York, it's a short trip but I need to switch all the cozy sweater vibes, for some pieces that are more fly and stylish." she said. "You can go to your hotel, relax and I'll text you my apartment address later so we can meet up. If that's cool with you?" she finally looked up from her phone.

"What?" She said.

"Sounds good," he said with a smile.

He wanted her to know He was not here to crowd her. He was here to be present.

Still, the thought hit him again, quiet and insistent. I'm in her city. By choice. The car pulled up in front of her grandmother's house. Brick. Modest. A wreath on the door. Icicles hanging from the roof like the house itself was dressed for winter.

Asha stepped out, and Rick stayed seated for a second longer than necessary, watching her.

"I'll see you in a bit," she said.

"I'll be around," he replied, softer than he intended.

She nodded and walked up the steps, her shoulders squared but her pace just a little too fast. Rick waited until she disappeared inside before the door closed. Only then did he exhale.

IF HE WAS HONEST, THE decision to get on that plane scared the hell out of him.

Less than twenty-four hours earlier, after the holiday noise had faded and Asha had gone upstairs to pack, Rick had found himself lingering in the Wintercrest kitchen with Ryan. He was wiping down counters that were already clean, pretending to help while his thoughts refused to settle.

"Which flight is she on?" he asked, casual enough that it almost sounded unplanned.

Ryan looked up slowly.

It was the kind of look that told him she already knew the answer to a question he had not asked out loud.

"You've got some nerve asking that," she said. "After whatever that was you pulled earlier."

Rick exhaled. "I know. And I didn't handle it right. But she didn't deserve that either."

Ryan crossed her arms, studying him. "Then what was it? Because from where I was standing, it looked like you two were getting to know each other."

He ran a hand over his face, frustration bleeding through. "I jumped to conclusions. I heard part of a conversation and filled in the rest with my own insecurity instead of just being honest."

That made her pause.

"She likes you," Ryan said simply. "And you like her. Stop acting like there's some rulebook for when you're allowed to feel that."

Rick frowned. "It's not that simple."

"It never is," she replied. "But listen to me. She wasn't obligated to explain her entire life to you on your timeline. She barely knew what she was doing herself."

He swallowed.

Ryan softened just a fraction, her voice steady but sure. "If you want to build something, you show up. You don't wait for perfect timing. You don't let fear make the decision for you."

The words settled deep. Heavy. Undeniable.

She slid her phone across the counter.

"Row fourteen. Seat B."

Rick stared at the screen, his pulse thudding loudly in his ears.

"You don't have to do this," Ryan added. "But if you do, do it because you mean it. Not because you're scared of losing her."

Rick nodded once.

"I'm not missing this."

LATER THAT EVENING, Rick stood outside Asha's apartment door, hands in his pockets, breathing slower than his body wanted to.

"Need help?" he asked when she opened the door.

"If you want to," she said, stepping aside.

He did.

Her apartment felt like her in a way that took him by surprise. Soft lighting. Cream throws. Plants everywhere. A space that looked intentional, like someone who knew how to build comfort and keep moving forward.

"This looks like you," he said quietly. "Soft. Organized. Busy. Pretty."

She shot him a look. "Did you just call my apartment pretty?"

He shrugged. "If the shoe fits."

They packed in an easy rhythm. Folding clothes. Charging batteries. Sorting memory cards. Rick found himself watching the way she worked, focused and precise, talking through her plans out loud like she was lining up her future one thought at a time.

She showed him her storyboard for Sirius Beatz, and he listened. Not because he was trying to impress her, but because he wanted to understand her. The choices. The vision. The care she put into things that mattered.

Somewhere between the storm, the kiss, and this quiet, almost domestic moment, he stopped pretending this was casual.

When they finished, he lingered by the door longer than necessary.

"Get some sleep," he said.

"I will."

"And don't lift that big suitcase alone," he added. "I'll grab it in the morning."

She smiled. "You're bossy."

"You like it."

He leaned in and kissed her cheek. Slow and deliberate. The moment stretched, fragile and unspoken. He stepped back before either of them reached for more than they were ready to offer.

"Goodnight, Asha."

"Goodnight, Rick."

She closed the door gently. Rick stayed there a bit longer than he should have, staring at the wood like it might give something back.

In a city that already belonged to her, something was shifting for him too. He didn't know where this would lead. He didn't know how fast or how far. But he was finally making a choice he wasn't second-guessing.

CHAPTER NINETEEN

New York had never been quiet to Rick. He'd learned its rhythms years ago. The early horns. The steam rising from grates like the city exhaling. The way mornings moved fast even when nothing urgent was happening. Noise didn't overwhelm him here. It grounded him.

What felt new was Asha standing in it.

She lingered outside the coffee shop he'd brought her to, manicured fingers wrapped around a paper cup that read City Grind in looping script. The cold nipped at her cheeks, her short stylish cut tucked neatly beneath her hat, eyes bright in that way they got when she was taking everything in at once.

Rick watched her without meaning to.

"This is better than I expected," she said after a sip.

He lifted his own cup. "I wouldn't bring you somewhere with weak coffee. That would be disrespectful."

She smiled, slow and pleased. "So, this is your spot."

"One of them," he said. "But it felt right for today."

Today.

The word carried more weight than he let on.

Sirius Beatz.

The shoot.

The thing that could change the direction of her life.

Rick was used to New York feeling like a checkpoint. A place people passed through on their way to whatever came next. But watching Asha stand there, vibrating with anticipation, made the city feel different.

More intentional.

More alive.

He clocked the tension in her shoulders even as she tried to play it cool.

"On a scale from one to ten," he asked, "how anxious are you?"

She didn't hesitate. "A strong fifteen. But my lip gloss looks good, so I'll survive."

He laughed, low and genuine. "You're about to do more than survive."

She glanced at him. "Oh yeah?"

"You are," he said. "You're about to kill this."

He didn't say it like encouragement. He said it like fact.

They weren't far from the studio. Just a few blocks, but enough time for Rick to settle into the rhythm of the city again.

He took Asha's arm and guided her into the current foot traffic, bodies moving with purpose around them. This part of New York didn't pause or apologize. People walked like they had somewhere to be. Rick moved easily through it, instinct taking over.

Wintercrest had softened his edges more than he'd realized. Here, he didn't hesitate. Didn't overthink. His fingers slid naturally between hers as they stepped around slush piles and impatient pedestrians, his grip firm without being restrictive.

Protective, even.

Asha looked around, eyes jumping from storefronts to scaffolding to the stretch of billboards overhead. "I still can't believe this is your world," she said. "Like... every day."

He smiled to himself. "Part of it. When I'm home."

She squeezed his hand once. "I like it."

Something warm shifted in his chest.

They turned onto a side street lined with brick buildings and metal roll-up doors, the kind that hid studios, offices, and small creative spaces behind unassuming fronts. A black SUV idled at the curb nearby. A few people stood outside smoking, phones pressed to ears, gear cases stacked against the wall.

Rick clocked the entrance immediately.

And the man leaning against it.

Tall. Black bomber jacket. Fitted beanie pulled low. Hands tucked into his pockets like he was exactly where he intended to be. The grin was already there, lazy and familiar, like trouble waiting to be entertained.

"There he is," Rick muttered, shaking his head. "Lord, give me strength."

Zavier spotted them and pushed off the wall. "Slick Rick!" he called out. "Look at you, surviving blizzards and pulling up with a woman who is clearly way too good for you."

Rick shot him a look. "Zavier. Don't."

Asha bit back a laugh. So, this was him.

Zavier pulled Rick into a quick hug, clapping him on the back. "Glad you made it, man."

Then his attention shifted fully to her.

"You must be Asha," he said. "Zavier Carter. Best friend. Better dressed. And according to Rick, the reason he never sleeps."

Asha arched a brow and glanced at Rick. "Non-stop, huh?"

Rick groaned. "Ignore him."

"I will not," she said easily. "Zavier, please continue. What else has your friend told you about me?"

Zavier's grin widened. "I live for this. First of all, I'm very glad you exist. Second, thank you for giving this man a reason to stop silently brooding like the world personally wronged him."

Asha laughed. "That's facts."

"Oh yeah," Zavier said, nodding. "I like you already."

He reached for her bag. "Come on, let me—"

Rick grabbed it first. "I got it."

Zavier smirked. "See? Learning."

Rick led them into the building, the warmth of the lobby closing in around them. Exposed brick. Industrial lighting. The low hum of city life still echoing faintly through the glass doors.

Zavier fell into step beside him. "I was already meeting Don about some party stuff nearby," he said quietly. "Figured I'd pull up. Thought it was time I met the woman who had you flying out to the Second City."

Rick glanced at Asha, then back at his friend. "Yeah," he said, mouth curving faintly. "It was."

Having Zavier here mattered. Not just because he trusted him, but because this city could chew people up if you didn't know how to move through it. Asha was capable. Fierce. But New York was different.

Rick stayed close as they headed toward the studio entrance.

His city.

His best friend.

Her world expanding in real time.

INSIDE, THE STUDIO smelled like hairspray, coffee, and expensive cologne. Organized chaos hummed through the room. Light stands. Cables. Music vibrating just enough to be felt.

Sirius Beatz was already there, laughing with his stylist near the wardrobe rack. Gold chains. Clean fade. Hoodie layered under a tailored coat.

"Asha Stewart," Sirius said when he saw her, arms wide. "The woman with the eye. I've been stalking your work."

"You are going to make me nervous," she said, laughing.

"Good," he replied. "Nervous people work harder."

A voice from the group leaned in and whispered to Asha, "Ms. Stewart, are they with you?" A few curious looks shifted toward Rick and Zavier.

Asha smiled. "Yep. Those are my guys. They're with me."

Rick watched the shift happen.

The moment she stepped forward, she was different. Focused. Grounded. In control. She checked lighting. Angles. Her shot list. Everything precise without being stiff.

Rick stayed just outside the main circle. Close enough. Out of the way. He handed her lenses before she asked. Adjusted a stand when it leaned. Every time she turned, he was already there.

Zavier disappeared into the rhythm of the shoot, flirting easily, making people laugh. Rick didn't need to see him to know he was nearby.

Hours blurred.

"Chin up. Just a little."

"Freeze."

"Less bravado. More quiet legend."

Sirius did exactly what she asked.

At one point, Sirius glanced from Asha to Rick. "That your man?"

Rick stiffened.

Asha nearly dropped her camera. "Who?"

Rick winced. They still hadn't named whatever this was.

Sirius nodded toward him. "The one watching you like you hung the moon."

Heat crept up her neck. "We're... figuring it out."

Sirius smiled. "Yeah. That's your man."

Rick looked away, but the truth settled in his chest, heavy and steady.

LATER, DURING A SHORT break, Rick and Zavier drifted toward the monitors where Asha stood with a woman Rick hadn't met yet. The two of them looked easy together, bodies angled in, laughing like they'd known each other for longer than a few hours.

The woman was tall and curvy, dressed in a bronze jumpsuit that caught the light every time she moved. Her braided ponytail fell sleek down her back, and her eyeliner was sharp enough to start a fight. She carried confidence like armor.

As Rick got closer, he heard the tail end of their conversation.

"You walked in here and the whole energy shifted," the woman was saying. "Sirius is already talking about bringing you in on the next rollout if this goes the way I think it will."

Asha's smile went wide, unguarded. "Seriously?"

"Seriously," the woman replied without hesitation. "Pun absolutely intended."

They laughed, then both looked up as Rick and Zavier approached.

"Rick. Zavier," Asha said, gesturing between them. "Meet Yasmine Cole. Creative Director for Sirius Beatz."

Rick nodded in greeting. Zavier leaned in with a grin. "Hey, Ms. Lady."

Yasmine smiled, amused, then turned her attention to Rick just as he handed Asha a bottle of water.

"So, what exactly does a creative director do?" Rick asked casually. "Besides intimidate rooms and make people nervous?"

Yasmine laughed. "Fair question." She folded her arms, considering. "Think of it like this—artists like Beyoncé, Kanye, Rihanna... they don't just wake up looking iconic by accident. Someone's shaping the vision. The look. The story people feel before the music even hits."

Rick nodded slowly.

"I'm the bridge," she continued. "Between brand, image, culture, and execution. I make sure everything aligns so when people see it, they feel it."

"And where does Asha come in?" Rick asked, glancing at her.

Yasmine didn't miss a beat. "She sees what most people miss. She doesn't just shoot pretty pictures. She understands identity. Messaging. Longevity." She looked at Asha with real warmth. "You give artists a visual language that actually matches who they are."

Rick watched Asha absorb that, watched her shoulders lift just a little with pride.

"That's why I need her," Yasmine added. "Not just for this shoot. For the bigger picture."

Rick clocked it then—this wasn't luck. This was who she was.

Zavier plopped into a chair nearby. "Okay, real question for the group. Is this New Year's Eve party going to be full of couples, or will single people like me be allowed to exist without judgment?"

Rick shook his head. "Bro, you are not single. You are dramatic."

"I am dramatically single," Zavier corrected. "There is a difference."

Yasmine sipped her coffee and raised a brow. "Wait. New Year's Eve party?"

Rick nodded. "My annual thing. Little rooftop situation. Some good music, good food. Nothing too wild. You're invited. Bring ya homegirls."

Asha smiled. "You should come through. It's a rooftop with the New York skyline. Can't beat that."

Yasmine sighed. "Hmm. I would love to go, but I am not showing up solo to a party like that. My ex lives in this city, and he happens to follow all the local DJs and parties like they pay him."

Asha's eyes lit with mischief. "So, what you're saying is, you need a date."

"Exactly," Yasmine said.

Asha turned to Rick. "Does your boy Zavier have plans?"

Rick narrowed his eyes. "Do not pimp my friend out to strangers."

Zavier sat up straighter. "First of all, I accept. Second, please baby pimp me out."

Yasmine looked him over, amused. "You this confident with everybody, or is it the haircut?"

"It is the whole package," Zavier replied. "But you are welcome to investigate."

Asha pressed her lips together to keep from laughing. Rick let out a groan.

"This is a bad idea," Rick muttered.

"Honestly? That's not terrible," Asha said. "A fake date at a rooftop party saves a lot of explanations."

Yasmine considered it for all of three seconds. "Alright, Zavier. You can be my date."

He placed a hand over his heart. "I will do my absolute best to pretend I am not having the time of my life."

Asha and Rick's eyes met. She grinned. "Look at that. We are fixing lives."

He shook his head, but there was a smile tugging at his mouth. "You are a mess."

"You like it," she said.

He did not argue.

THE CITY FINALLY GAVE them a pause.

No call times.

No alarms.

No calendar reminders blinking for attention.

Just the low hum of traffic outside his windows and Asha curled into his side like she'd been there longer than a few days.

Rick leaned back into the couch, one arm draped along the backrest, the other resting loosely at her waist. She sat cross-legged beside him, laptop balanced easily on her knees, her shoulder brushing his arm every time she shifted.

This was new for him. Not the quiet. Not the closeness. But the ease.

Asha edited photos and video clips in silence, fingers flying over the keys, pausing every so often to squint at the screen or tilt her head like she was negotiating with a memory. Rick watched her more than the TV playing something he wasn't really paying attention to.

She was in her zone. Comfortable. At home in his space. That mattered more than he wanted to admit. His phone buzzed on the coffee table.

Sullivan.

Rick reached for it, careful not to move her too much.

"Yo," he said quietly.

"Checking in," Sullivan replied. "You alive over there?"

Rick smiled faintly. "Barely."

"Good sign," Sullivan said. "You see the calendar update?"

"Yeah," Rick said. "Check your email too. I added a couple tour dates and set up a meeting with the owner of Basinger Books."

Asha glanced up from her laptop, interest flickering across her face. Rick caught it, the way she noticed his tone shifting into work mode.

Sullivan paused. "Hold on...Basinger? We've been trying to get that meeting all year."

"His assistant finally got back to me," Rick said. "Said there was an opening if we could be flexible."

"Ok, that's what's up. Looking forward to this one. "Sullivan paused for a second. "Aight then."

Rick waited.

"Brandy and I are spending New Year's with my mom in Pinehill," Sullivan continued. "So, enjoy that woman of yours and do not party too hard."

Rick huffed a quiet laugh. "You say that like I'm reckless."

"You are," Sullivan said easily. "We got cities to hit."

Rick smiled. "I'll keep it light."

"Good man," Sullivan said. "We'll sync after the holiday."

"Bet," Rick replied.

Rick set the phone back on the table and exhaled.

"You really like being behind the scenes," she said.

"I like making things move," he replied. "Even if nobody sees it."

She smiled. "I see it."

Something warm settled in him. Not overwhelming. Just steady.

Asha turned her laptop slightly toward him. "Look at this."

It was a photo from Wintercrest. Snow piled high behind them, cabin lights glowing soft and gold. And there he was. Arms crossed. Jaw tight. Brows furrowed like the world had personally offended him.

Rick groaned. "Why do I look mad at air?"

She laughed, leaning back into his chest. "You were pissed off."

"I was just a little upset," he corrected.

"A little upset? Ha! You came in like our total existence offended you."

"Also, true."

She tilted her head to look up at him. "You hated it."

"At first," he admitted. "I don't love being stuck."

"And now?"

He thought about it. About the snowball fight. The pie. The way everything slowed just enough to let him feel things he usually outran.

"And now I'm glad I got stuck."

Her smile softened. She closed the laptop and set it aside.

Rick hesitated, then shifted forward, reaching toward the side table. He grabbed a thin folder, slightly bent at the corners, like it had been opened and closed more times than he wanted to admit.

"Asha," he said.

She raised a brow. "What's that, Franklin?"

He shot her a look. "Do not call me that while I'm being vulnerable."

She grinned. "Too late."

He handed her the folder. "It's... something I've been working on."

She opened it, eyes scanning the first page.

"A screenplay?" she asked.

"Don't read the ending," he said quickly. "Or the middle. Or judge the formatting."

She laughed. "Sir. I read books. I can handle pages."

She tucked her legs under herself, fully turning toward him now. Laptop forgotten. Phone silent. Just him.

That alone made his chest feel exposed. She read quietly. Occasionally humming. Occasionally making a face like something clicked. Ten minutes passed. Then twenty. Rick tried to play it cool. Failed.

"You're squinting," she said without looking up.

"I'm breathing," he replied.

She flipped a page. "Barely."

An hour later, she closed the folder gently.

Rick waited.

"Well?" he asked.

She leaned back, studying him. "You're a nervous wreck."

He exhaled. "Cool."

"But," she added quickly, "it's good."

He blinked. "Good how?"

"Good like I can see it," she said. "I can hear it. The pacing makes sense. The characters feel lived-in. It's funny in a quiet way. Observational."

She tilted her head. "I didn't know you had this in you."

He swallowed. "Neither did I."

She scooted closer, resting her shoulder against his chest again. "I'm not a professional, but as someone who loves stories... this works."

He let his head fall back against the couch.

"Thank you," he said quietly.

She smiled. "I already have ideas."

He turned to her. "Of course you do."

"You need a brand," she said. "Not just a script. You need a presence. Mood. Visuals. A way for people to get you before they read you."

Rick stared at her. "You're doing it again."

"Doing what?"

"Seeing me."

She shrugged. "You deserve it."

That did something to him. He tightened his arm around her, pulling her closer. She fit. Easy. Like this rhythm had been waiting on them. For the first time in a long time, Rick didn't feel like he had to choose between ambition and connection.

Maybe this thing...whatever it was, wasn't a distraction. Maybe it was fuel. And for once, he didn't feel the urge to run from it.

CHAPTER TWENTY

The rooftop looked like the inside of a champagne bottle. Gold lights hung in cascading strings from beams overhead. Candles glowed on cocktail tables. A soft mix of R&B and gentle trap soul rolled through the air, wrapping the crowd in something warm and easy.

The city stretched in every direction. Bridges lit up in the distance. Snow fell in a light, cinematic drift, just enough to sparkle without ruining anyone's hair.

Asha stepped out of the elevator and paused; one hand still curled around the strap of her clutch. She didn't move right away. Just stood there, letting it land.

This wasn't just a party.

It felt intentional. Thought through. Like someone had imagined how it should feel and then made it real.

She smoothed her palm down the side of her dress, more to ground herself than anything else.

Black. Body-hugging. Slipping just off her shoulders, tracing every curve like it had been made with her in mind. Pearls glimmered at her neck, matched by delicate studs that sparkled each time she turned her head. A soft pixie cut framed her face, effortless in a way that made people look twice without knowing why.

People laughed near the bar. Couples leaned into each other for photos beneath a glowing "Happy New Year" arch. Zavier and Yasmine were already posted up in a corner, fake dating a little too convincingly. He leaned in to say something low in her ear. She threw her head back laughing, one hand resting easily on his chest.

Asha smiled to herself.

And then she saw him.

Rick stood near the center of the rooftop, half-turned toward the DJ, listening while the man talked through the midnight set. Charcoal blazer. Black dress shirt, open at the collar. No tie. Clean lines. Easy confidence: that didn't ask for attention but somehow held it anyway.

City lights reflected faintly in his eyes as he nodded, asked a question, adjusted something on the table.

He looked settled here. Like the city had finally loosened its grip on him instead of demanding something. She forgot, briefly, what she'd been about to do. Different, she thought. Not changed. Just... expanded.

Still the man who had argued with her in a blizzard. Still the one who'd held her hand on a snowy road like it was the most natural thing in the world. Still chaos and comfort braided together in a way she hadn't learned how to resist yet.

As if he felt her staring, Rick turned. Their eyes met across the rooftop. The music softened. The chatter dulled. Everything else receded, leaving just the two of them standing still in a moving crowd.

Something familiar slid neatly back into place. That quiet pull that had survived snowstorms, tow trucks, pecan pie, and airports. Not loud. Not frantic. Just there. Rick didn't move right away.

He finished listening. Said something quick to the DJ. Tapped the table once, like punctuation. Then he turned fully and started toward her.

Each step felt deliberate. Unrushed. Asha adjusted the camera strap on her shoulder, pretending she needed to. Shifted her weight. Reminded herself to breathe normally, even as her pulse picked up its own rhythm.

"You clean up nice, Franklin," she said when he stopped in front of her, aiming for casual and landing somewhere close.

His mouth curved, slow and unmistakable. "So do you."

The words were quiet, but the way he said them lingered.

She brushed her hand down the front of her dress again, the fabric catching light as she moved. The camera strap rested against her shoulder, familiar and grounding. Even tonight, wrapped in champagne glow and city magic, she couldn't help herself.

He noticed. Always did.

"You ready for this?" he asked, eyes searching her face instead of the crowd.

She glanced around, taking it all in again. The lights. The music. The people already leaning toward midnight.

"My answer depends," she said. "Your party? The shoot? The next year? Or all the above?"

"All of it," he said, without hesitation.

She looked back at him. Really looked.

"Yeah," she said, warmth spreading low and steady through her chest. "I think I am."

Rick nodded once, like he'd been waiting for that exact answer.

"Good," he said softly. "Come on. Let me show you around."

And just like that, he slipped his hand lightly at her back, guiding her forward into the glow, into the noise, into the night that was about to change everything.

THE NEXT HOUR MOVED fast.

Asha worked the rooftop like it was second nature. Sliding through the crowd. Catching laughter mid-sip. Pulling couples closer to the lights without breaking their rhythm. She adjusted angles on instinct, lifted her camera, lowered it again, waited for the exact right second.

Rick stayed in motion beside her. Not hovering. Not leading. Just there. He checked in with the caterer when trays ran low, leaned in with the DJ about timing, gave security a quick nod when the crowd pressed closer to the rail. Every time Asha shifted back without looking, his hand landed at her elbow, steady and sure.

"Careful," he murmured once, already guiding her out of someone's path.

She glanced up at him. "You trying to keep me alive?"

"Trying to keep you working," he said. "Big difference."

She smiled and lifted her camera again.

They didn't stop to define anything. Didn't pause to name what this was. They moved like people who already knew each other's patterns. Like this wasn't new, just newly visible.

At the bar, she leaned into the counter beside him, scrolling through shots while the bartender refilled glasses nearby.

"Oh, this one's fire," she said, turning the screen toward him. "Look at that framing."

Rick studied it, then her. "That's all you."

She shook her head. "Nah. You set the whole thing up. The lighting. The flow. The vibe." She nudged his arm. "Don't act brand new."

He laughed under his breath. "Fine. Team effort."

"See? You're learning."

He raised a brow. "Am I getting graded?"

"Absolutely," she said. "And so far, you're passing."

He leaned closer, lowering his voice. "What do I get if I ace it?"

She didn't look up from her camera. "A surprise."

"Sounds like an interesting reward," he said.

She finally met his eyes.

Around them, the rooftop hummed. Glasses clinked. Music swelled and dipped. People leaned into midnight without realizing how close it already was.

"We're good together," he said, not loud, not dramatic. Just stated, like something he'd already tested and decided was true.

She held his gaze for a beat longer than necessary. "Yeah," she said. "We are."

She didn't say anything else. Didn't need to.

The way he stepped aside to let her catch another shot. The way she reached for him without thinking when she laughed. The way neither of them felt rushed to move on.

That was enough.

A LITTLE BEFORE ELEVEN fifty, Asha slipped out onto the side balcony. She needed air, but not because of the crowd.

Her camera rested against her hip. Below, the city stretched wide and lit, windows stacked like constellations. In the distance, a few test fireworks cracked and fizzled, bright and brief.

Rick joined her a moment later, coat unbuttoned, breath visible in the cold. He leaned against the railing beside her, close enough to feel without touching.

"You did good tonight," Asha said, still looking out at the skyline. "This party is kind of perfect."

He angled toward her, "You showing up made it that way."

She felt the warmth of him even through the chill. She turned her head, catching his eyes in the low light.

"You know, for someone who swears he's bad at saying how he feels, you've been doing alright lately." A corner of his mouth lifted.

"I meant what I said on the plane. I'm where you are. If you want me there."

He didn't rush it. Didn't fill the space with extra words. He just waited. Her thoughts moved fast and slow all at once. Wintercrest. The cabin. Snowbanks and tow trucks. The pecan pie kiss. Chicago streets. This rooftop. His hand finding hers like it already knew the way.

"I do," she said. Quiet, steady. "I want you here."

His shoulders eased, the tension she hadn't realized he was holding finally slipping free.

"Okay," he murmured.

He didn't reach for her. She didn't close the distance. They stayed exactly where they were, letting the weight of it settle, letting it feel real. From inside, the DJ's voice rose, calling people closer, pulling the party inward.

"Ten minutes," Rick said.

Asha took one last look at the city, then at him. "Let's go start the year right."

He smiled, offering his hand this time.

She took it.

THE ROOFTOP SLOWLY drew everyone inward. The DJ lowered the lights, and the city noise faded into something distant, replaced by a soft, pulsing beat that felt like a shared breath being held.

Zavier and Yasmine claimed a spot near the front, still playing their roles a little too convincingly. Rick and Asha stopped near the rail, close enough to see the glowing countdown clock reflected on the DJ's screen.

Phones lifted.

Glasses tipped.

The crowd pressed closer.

"Ten."

Rick's fingers threaded through hers, sure and deliberate, like he'd done it a thousand times already.

"Nine."

He turned toward her fully, his body creating a quiet pocket of space just for them.

"Eight."

The light caught his face, warm and gold, softening the edges she knew so well.

"Seven."

"Tell me if I'm reading this wrong," he murmured, close enough that only she could hear him.

"Six."

Her breath hitched, but she didn't look away.

"Five."

She rose slightly onto her toes, closing the distance without touching.

"Four."

"You're not," she whispered.

"Three."

His hand found her waist, steady and grounding, like an anchor.

"Two."

Her fingers curled into his jacket, holding him there.

"One."

The rooftop exploded.

Cheers rose. Fireworks bloomed over the skyline. Champagne popped and spilled. Music surged back to life.

Rick kissed her. No hesitation. No doubt. It was slow and certain, that carried intention without needing to say a word. A kiss built on shared looks, missed chances, and choosing each other anyway.

She melted into him, her hand finding his jaw, the texture of him beneath her fingertips. His arm wrapped around her, pulling her close, not as if to claim her, but as if he already belonged there.

Everything else fell away. When they finally pulled back, they stayed close, foreheads touching, smiles breaking through soft laughter.

"Happy New Year, Asha," he said, voice low and full.

She looked at him like she was still catching her breath. "Happy New Year, Rick."

His thumb brushed along her jaw, unhurried. "So... you and me. This year."

She answered without thinking, without fear. "You and me."

And on a rooftop in New York, with the city glowing and the year turning beneath their feet, Asha stepped forward into something she'd never planned for.

Not carefully. Not safely. But fully. With him.

Thank You for Reading!

R ead more from the Sweet Seasons Holiday Romance Collection. These books can be read as standalones or in release order. Reading order, book links, visuals, and bonus goodies: www.authorninastewart.com

Sweet Potato Kisses: A Friendsgiving Romance

A Friends-to-Lovers, Holiday Small-Town Vibes, Cozy Slow Burn. ISBN: 979-8-218-87469-8

Pecan Pie For Two: A Christmas Romance

An Enemies-to-Lovers, Snowed-In Forced Proximity, Cozy Slow Burn: ISBN 979-8-218-91529-2

Something to Savor: A New Year's Eve to Remember

Fake Dating, New Year's Romance, Opposites-Attract Energy

About The Author

Nina Stewart is a native of Chicago, Illinois, who also proudly considers Minneapolis, Minnesota her home. She is a mother of three, an Army service member, and a lifelong storyteller. Nina wrote her first books at the age of eight "Get Well Soon, Grandma" and "Me and My Little Sister Bo Bo." Even then, she knew stories were her way of loving the world.

Nina writes clean, no-spice romance because she wanted love stories that celebrate chemistry, connection, and the soft, slow beginning of falling in love without explicit scenes. Her books capture warmth, friendship, and the magic of Black love, often wrapped in cozy, holiday vibes.

When she's not writing, Nina enjoys baking, crafting, and watching every Hallmark holiday movie she can find.

You can connect with her at:

TikTok: authorninastewart

Instagram: authorninastewart

Facebook: Author Nina Stewart

Website: www.authorninastewart.com

Business inquiries: theauthorstrategist@gmail.com